Drive By

Shards & Poems

By John Bennett

ISBN 978-1-929878-09-3

First edition

Lummox Press
PO Box 5301
San Pedro, CA 90733
www.lummoxpress.com

Printed in the United States of America

Some of these Shards and poems have appeared in the following hard-copy and on-line magazines and anthologies: Arabesque; Big Hammer; Black Rabbit Press; East/West; First Class; Heavy Bear; Measured Steps/Kirpan Press; Mystery Island; Ol Chanty; OpEd News; Outsider Writer; Private Poetry Line; Pudding House; Smoken Word (sic); Unlikely Stories

Table of Concepts:

Table of Concepts *continued*

A Rare Moment in Warfare

The chieftain came
riding out of
the trees &
across the
corpse-strewn
field in Germania,
bareback on a
candy-striped
unicorn.

The Roman general
raised an arm,
& the archers
held their fire.

Substitute

When my father
was one of
six children
& the
bills were
piling up
his father
walked out
the door &
never came back.

The new
father was
Irish &
feisty
had a
strong sense
of justice &
no education.

He could
lift a
broom by
its handle
with
ten books
piled on
the bristles

used the
belt freely
could not
stand a lie
was obeyed but
seldom loved.

A pipe fitter
by trade
he spent the
rest of
his life
in the
bowels of a
big New York
hotel
descending
daily into
heat &
darkness.

He died
one April a
shriveled
substance of
gray the
hospital
window
open
trees &
flowers in

bloom &
the cries of
stick ball
on the
street below.

The last
thing to die
was a
question in
his eyes
answered by
my father's
tears his
great head
descending to
the
shock-white
sheets.

Death is Dancing All Around Me

I told her to call anytime of the day or night if she needed me, and she did. I rolled out of bed and threw on some clothes and drove over there.

He'd taken the oxygen tube in his nose for a catheter and wet the bed. She'd managed to get him up and into a recliner while she changed the bedding, but then he couldn't get up again--his legs just stopped working.

When I got there he was giving orders like he always does but he was also sliding in and out of different realities, talking to his father who's been dead for years, taking stock of his water supply and seeing that they needed to lay in a case of spring water from Safeway, calculating that what needed doing right now was to push the recliner across the room to the side of the bed, and from there he could pull himself up and in.

I leaned over him and said, "Better would be if I bend over and you lock your hands around my neck and I walk you to the bed."

"It won't work," he said, panic in his voice, his eyes wide, his skin gray and smooth as a baby's. "We need to get everything in place," he said. "I need to be sure it's right."

"It's right," I said. "We're good to go."

"Are you sure?" he said.

"Hell yes," I said. "So latch on now and let's do it."

"I'm in a lot of places at once," he said, and I said, "I know."

"That's right," he said, remembering, and he locked his hands around my neck.

I got him back in bed. I convinced him that he didn't have a catheter up his nose, how silly would that be? His wife gave him two pills, one for the pain and one to knock him out cold, and then we stepped back into the shadows of the dimmly-lit high-ceilinged room, the walls covered with the art that he'd created over the years. She broke down then, cried quietly, and I held her and stroked her hair.

Death is dancing all around me, suicides and cancer, and just a couple of years ago I was right there where my friend is now, except he won't make it back. The most terrifying thing about being in that place is that people around you start thinking you've lost touch with reality, when in fact you're deeper into reality than they can possibly imagine. He'd seen me in that place, and the panic left his eyes when he remembered. He put his arms around my neck, and together we struggled across the room to his final resting place.

I Don't Speak German

I ran into them at a party, a husband and wife team. He teaches German at one university, she teaches it at another. They hail from San Diego, but they speak flawless high German, all their declensions in perfect order.

The husband was going on about their recent trip to Germany, how he corrected the German of native speakers in Munich, Dresden and Bremen, waitresses and streetcar conductors and porters. They were speaking English at the party of course, but now and then they'd throw in a six-syllable German word to intimidate anyone present who thought they knew a little German themselves.

And then the woman I was with blurted out, "He speaks German!" She meant me.

The German-language professors turned their heads slowly in my direction, like cannon turrets on the Siegfried Line.

"Oh?" the husband said. *"Sprechen Sie Deutsch?"*

I stared at him.

"Did you understand my question?" he said. "I asked if you speak German."

I lit a cigarette and blew out some smoke. *"Du bist ein Arschloch,"* I said, and his smile faded.

Everyone around the table was beaming. A real conversation in German was about to get underway.

"Wie, bitte?" the husband said. He couldn't believe his ears.

"You heard me," I said. "You're an asshole. You don't speak German, you speak German words. Talk to me after you've had to talk down six German riot police who've just kicked in your door. After you've done a ten-hour shift washing dishes in a Munich restaurant and are riding home on the *Strassenbahn* talking German with a Turkish co-worker, the only language you have in common. After you've picked up your four-year-old son from your parents in Newport News where you left him for a month, your son who's never spoken anything but German, and while walking to the corner and back with him, trying to explain how things got so fucked up and why you left him alone in a strange house in a strange land with strange people, he cuts you off and in heavily-accented English says, 'I don't schpeak German. Schpeak me in English,' and you can't say anything in any language for the lump in your throat..."

There was silence after that. And then the husband said, "Try saying all that in German. I'll bet you make thirty grammatical errors."

Everyone at the table looked down, except the man's wife, who was staring at him as if she'd never seen him before. "He's right, Carl," she said. "You're an asshole."

I got up from the table and walked out onto the patio and across the dark lawn, that lump in my throat from so long ago back again, as if no time had gone by at all.

Hot Flashes of Life

So I opted for
local anesthetic &
an I.V. drip
power-packed with
Fentanyl &
some high-grade
Valium
that zonked me out
so heavy I
may as well have
been out
all the way,
except I did
surface from
time to time,
& there
as if in a
dream was my
elfish Irish surgeon
bent over me
& intent on
his work.
The blonde nurse
from the
prep room was
there too,
& even in such
dire straits
I got a
sexual hit.
Somewhere out of
sight was the
bearded rotund
anesthesiologist

with a
head-wrap bandanna
that made him
look like a
Hell's Angel,
& after lingering
half conscious
for a while I
mumbled,
"Kick it up a
notch, dude."
& apparently he
did, because the
next thing I
knew I was
back on the
pre-op bed,
my ex taking
pictures with her
cell phone.
I immediately began
hamming it up,
& within two
hours I was
out of there.

In the middle
of the
first night
my body started
jerking around
in fits of
pain that
Percocet
couldn't touch,
& two days

later I was
on the
bathroom floor in
more pain still,
vomiting &
self-administering a
handy-pack enema
from Safeway &
swilling down a
vile laxative
concoction,
admonishing my ex
between groans
thru the
bathroom door
NOT to call
for an ambulance,
hospitals are the
8th highest cause
of death
in the country.

I went in today
for a
check-up,
& when the
surgeon
stripped off the
bandages,
there was his
handy work,
a series of
precision
incisions.
The reason the
whole thing

took two & a
half hours
instead of the
projected 45
minutes is that
when he
got in there
he found
the work from
the prior operation,
done by a
cardiovascular genius
from India,
in shambles--
mesh bent over
& torn loose
so that in
addition to
sewing up two
sizable hernias,
the Irish elf
had to open up
everything old &
start from
scratch.

I'm on the
hill now
with my
mocha &
cigarettes,
under instructions
to do
no more than
feels comfortable,
which, I'm learning

the hard way,
means in my
case one half
of what
feels comfortable,
because I
get these
hot flashes
of life
like right now
where I want to
jump out of
the car &
dance along the
cliff's edge
blasting away
on my
blues harp.
I want to
rock every
beautiful
woman I
lay eyes on
in my arms &
I want to
rip into a
new novel
& I want to
gather all the
wounded people
in my life
around me &
flood them
with whatever
this is
that surges

thru me like a
mountain stream
rushing madly
over rocks &
thru gullies
to be
swallowed
by the sea.

Madame Curie's Lap Dog

I am Madame Curie's lap dog, a timid isotope in a kennel of isotopes, my nose to the chain link, my whole focus on the lab door, waiting for it to swing wide and the grand lady herself to pass through. I'm longing to be chosen, placed under a microscope, longing to be probed and split and split again.

Chain link, chain reaction, missing link--the universe of awareness is made up of inference and fusion and cagey connections, all of it leading to silence.

Madame Curie was on to us, so we made her glow in the dark and then vanish.

I Am the Walrus

I am the walrus. You can be whatever you choose. A penguin, perhaps. Together we can learn to tap dance and join the Freaks & Oddities Show working its way north from Pensacola. We don't have to have sex. We can keep it platonic. Read the same book by candlelight lying side by side sipping red wine in our trailer. Let people talk.

I know I'm much older, but what's age to a penguin and a walrus? We know what's passed between us.

Years from now, after the novelty's worn off, we can adopt. If we're rejected, we can kidnap something--a partridge, a pheasant, a cockatoo. Birds of a feather, we'll stick together until the end.

This is what Joseph Campbell meant by follow your bliss.

Original Sin

It's as if we're born angels, and those who came before us put a pillow over our faces after they've tucked us into bed and hold it there until our tiny feet stop kicking. When they lift the pillow again we're one of them, our eyes vacant.

There are some who see this coming and stop kicking before they have to, so that when the pillow is lifted the angel inside still lives.

There's a heavy price to pay when you hang on to awe and wonder past a certain point. You're trapped in a world of vacant people who don't know they were once angels.

In such a world you only know peace when you're alone, or when a little girl skips by in a Safeway aisle, one blue sock, one red and her laces undone, smiling as if all the world were just like her.

The Boy with the Blue Mohawk

A jar of pickled ears. A delicacy in some parts of the world, mostly in war zones. Pain is just a feeling. It's what we think about it that makes us suffer. Witness a boy with a blue Mohawk and 200 piercings, seven through his genitals, the blank look in his eyes, a way to rise above childhood.

From here we could go in many directions at once, like a heretic being drawn and quartered. Noel, noel, Christ was born on Christmas Day, and he dared to differ.

The boy with the Mohawk differs in a different way, but he suffers the same. His father came back from an exotic war with a jar of pickled ears, and the two of them got drunk one night and ate each and every one in a vain attempt at bonding. It didn't work, and then came the piercings.

We draw and quarter our children and they retaliate with mutilation.

He Tried to Consider His Options

On his way to school in the brisk Kansas mornings he'd hum, "I've got rhythm, I've got music, who could ask for anything more?"

He wanted to be another Art Blakey, but before he got any further than clanging the cymbals together in the high-school marching band, Jean got pregnant in the back seat of his cherry-red Ford coupe. He dropped out of school, sold his drum set, and went to work as a mechanic for the Ford dealership.

He and Jean raised four children, and as soon as the last one moved out, Jean began talking about his drinking. It caught him off guard, and all he could think to say was, "I never missed a single day's work."

That wasn't good enough for Jean. "Normal people don't drink a six-pack a day and a pint of Jim Beam on weekends," she said, and told him he needed to go to A.A.

He went, and when it was his turn to talk he said, "I'm Art Blakey and I'm an alcoholic," even though he didn't believe it, the alcoholic part.

Jean started going to Al-Anon and saying things like, "All these years of enabling you, all these years of being a co-dependent. I can't take it no more. I need to get in touch with my inner child." It was like she'd learned a foreign language over night.

He had no idea what she was talking about. He stopped going to A.A. and started going to the local tavern instead, something he hadn't done more than a handful of times in all the years they'd been married.

Jean took his going to taverns as a sure sign that his disease was progressing, and her support group at Al-Anon told her that hard love was the only answer. He came home one Friday after work and found a note on the kitchen counter saying that his life was unmanageable and she'd gone off to find herself and not to come looking for her.

He took the Jim Beam out to his pick-up and sat in the dark drinking. He tried to consider his options, but by the time he'd finished the Jim Beam he'd gone numb and just stared out the windshield.

Economic Crisis

The way change jingles in your pocket when your billfold's empty. Credit-card free, you gear into grand-theft auto. Even with burn marks on your face, women give you the come on.

This is more than a roll. Life begins turning on a dime. Something inside floats to the surface like seaweed. You think about phoning home and then shine it on. She can have the house and the acreage and the mortgage, the summer place on the ocean.

You rent a room down on the waterfront and sit at the dark window smoking, knowing that you'll never again be confused.

Hanging on to the Handlebars

I can barely manage to hang on to the handlebars in this crashbar helmeted seatbelt world of seven-year plans and sudden death, this high-tone faster faster the lights are turning red merry-go-round of perpetual war and mental breakdown.

Foggy mountains and slow curves with no guard rails.

Interception, contraception, flared perception through a shattered prism.

Black visions of truth, white visions of easy come, a past gnawed away like a fox foot in a steel trap.

Home free and legless to parade into nowhere, rugged individuals waving tiny flags out front of a corporate White House.

Wrap up your troubles in swaddling and leave them on the first motherless doorstep you come to.

Rush headlong into happy hour and drown your sorrows straight into last call.

Night Train

This is not the train I rode in on. Those are not my original fellow passengers who are scurrying down the platform to the taxi stand. That man coming down the aisle sounding the dinner chime is not the conductor who took my ticket and turned back the sheets in my Pullman berth. This is not the destination they promised when they cried out, "All Aboard!"

In the box cars strung out behind this Silver Streak of rare fortune are faces more familiar. A rough mix of Gypsies and Jews, underage boys from Guatemala and old-fashioned hobos. Up in sleeping-car first class I can hear them rustling in their wool overcoats, coughing roughly in the thick air, trying one more time to turn straw into gold.

No matter how many times I throw cold water on my face in the uni-sex, my cheeks remain flushed.

The train pulls out of the station and gains speed, and gradually my face appears in the night window, a wavering apparition.

A Day Will Come

He entered the club house wearing a bright red tie held in place by a brass clip.

His skin color was passable, but the birthmark tangled in his left eyebrow was suspect.

And his pants were all wrong, baggy and stained. But creased, you had to give him that, and with cuffs.

His shoes spoke of great wealth, but his socks were checkered.

He wore a monocle, and on his bird's-egg-blue jacket, the Legion's medal of valor.

They couldn't just throw him out, but did they have to serve him?

Standing there in the doorway with the day blazing behind him, he gave them time to take it all in. Then he walked straight to the bar and sat down.

Hollyhocks

Make sense of a sunbeam, calculate a wave, calibrate a wolf howl, draw lines in the dust, go grim with a rifle defending the motherland, fatherland, land on your feet and start running, the hounds bay and the fox hunt is on.

Back and forth between the particular and the germane like a praying mantis lost in a butcher shop, cowboys and cowgirls riding side-saddle into the arena, gladiators peering through slits in spiked helmets, who do you love? Is it me, could it possibly be after all these years of false starts, heaps of gutted crab piled high in the corner?

I've got things gone amiss in life, a granddaughter gone astray, a lover with her arms crossed in a pout, a trick knee, heart, pony, imagination off in the ditch, tangled in carnage and confetti.

I wake with a whistle, slap my head and hop to it, I've still got a trick up my sleeve. Secrets intact I skip out the door into my rat-trap conveyance and with lights blinking red all around me roar off. "Java, java, java," I think, my life reduced to a coffee bean. "Plunk your magic twanger," I think, my vocabulary shrouded in code, ancient kid shows on the radio displacing Nietzsche and Kant. Hi-ho, hi-ho, off we go with the first cigarette of the day burning bright like a blowtorch between my once kissable lips.

The first rig at the drive-thru, the glass slides back and there they are, three blond beauties, a wild crazy perfection that drops death to its knees.

"Ho!" I sing out and trigger delight in them. They all three dance and glide to the window like goldfish in a pond, as if we'd just met in a dream.

"What'll it be?" says the tall one, and "Yes indeed!" I say. "What *will* it be!" Then we're lost for words as the universe sings all around us and hollyhocks wave in the morning breeze.

How to Win the Race

His mood changes from day to day, even as his tobacco runs short and his coffee slides into decaf. There he goes now, high as a kite, swinging like a crazed chimp through the top branches of his own chosen jungle. His mind is a tangle of feelings, there's no room left for a single thought to squeeze through. He's coming down the home stretch of a Grand-Prix existence on a road scarred with skid marks.

He breaks the tape with arms flung wide, chest out and head back, like Roger Bannister breaking the four-minute mile, something no one's done before and that he's now rendered commonplace.

Top Secret

He was shorter than Hitler and had no facial hair to speak of, but he could puff out his chest and fly into rages, and so they appointed him Leader. Elections had long since been abolished for reasons of national security, and a Leader and his cabinet members were routinely appointed by a self-perpetrating corporate board.

Before his appointment, everything including the lunch menu was classified Top Secret, but once in power he issued a decree that (because of its highly sensitive nature) only he was privy to, that it was Top Secret that everything was Top Secret. This triggered drastic repercussions.

Soon cabinet members as well as members of the corporate board were being whisked away in the dead of night by death squads from the Leader's Top Secret private-sector army for refusing to show their files to investigating committees of a titular congress, declaring them Top Secret: in so doing, they violated the Leader's Top Secret decree that it was Top Secret that everything was Top Secret.

The Leader, short and hairless though he was, was no fool. With a single decree he'd abolished government, broken the back of corporate power, and become supreme ruler without a shred of evidence available to prove that anything had changed.

He ruled until he died at the age of 89, at which time the country erupted in chaos.

Triple X

The face before it gets to the mirror. The face buried in the pillow to muffle the sharp cries of sex with a stranger. The face that is a whirlpool of Emptiness. *Us. Them. People. Elle.* These are the fashions with which we gloss things over.

The El, a sky ride to the next low-paying job. A little side trip while I catch my breath for round two--stop the bleeding, cauterize the wound, put on the mascara. For a transplanted Puerto Rican, the El is an adjective until he puts his token in the slot and takes the ride that shatters his heritage.

My distant past is showing, like the slip of a rape victim. Along the way I learned some grammar, I could decline with the best of them, but they sent me packing. Here, dig this ditch, they said. Dig that long row of potatoes. Skin the cat, file this top-secret document. Somehow I missed out on the lion's share, and now my shelf life is past pull date.

The war on porn, drugs, cigarettes--these things are almost virtues. The real war is on our looking up too fast and seeing what we're not supposed to. Even baby food is Triple X under the bright shiny label.

The Day the Wall Came Down

His name was Casanova Valentino Friedrich Don Juan Sabella. His friends called him Cassy. He didn't have many friends, mostly old men over eighty and widows. He was a lover.

It wasn't clear if it was his name that made him such. It wasn't even known that was his name until a reporter from *Elle* did the footwork and tracked it down through the *Standesamt* in Berlin. His father was an Italian Gypsy, his mother a German aristocrat.

He was sixteen when the wall came down. He strolled into West Berlin with the clothes on his back and sat down at a table at an outdoor café while the streets swirled in pandemonium. He made eye contact with a well-dressed middle-aged woman sitting over an espresso a few tables away, and they left together without exchanging a word.

He'd been at it since he was thirteen. He just did it, like eating and breathing.

***

The well-dressed woman who was waiting for him when he crossed over into the West was different. She had him sit next to her on the piano bench while she played Bartok. He'd never heard such music. He'd heard almost no music at all, except what came through the attic floorboards at night and strands of popular tunes that wafted out of *Gasthäuser* as he wandered the streets.

When he was seven, his father drifted back to Italy, and his mother, disowned by her family when she bore a Gypsy child out of wedlock, went from singing and dancing to the Gypsy's accordion in bistros to prostitution. A year later her throat got slit by a deranged john, and at the age of eight, Cassy became a ward of the bordello.

The women in the bordello fed him and kept him dressed in the Gypsy clothes he was accustomed to. He slept on a cot in the attic. He could neither read nor write. His first woman was a young girl from the bordello. After that there was a steady stream, some young, some old, some married, some not, some mothers of children no older than he was. He was a sex savant. He was legend.

The woman at the piano played Bartok, and by the time she'd finished, he was trembling. She led him into her tile and marble bathroom, bathed him like a child, and dried him with a blue Turkish towel. She took him to a tailor and a barber. She transformed him into a young man of fashion, and on the night of the day that the wall came down, he was her escort at a fashionable restaurant.

It went on like that until he reached the age of twenty, and in that time he learned to read and write. He became skilled in the social graces, and then, as she always knew he would, he left.

***

He made his way to Los Angeles where he became a gigolo. His picture appeared on all the tabloid covers with famous women in compromising situations. He was a guest on talk shows and got bit parts in movies. He went by the name of Willard Trent. And then the reporter from *Elle* tracked down his origins and discovered his real name.

The discovery was a news sensation. It overshadowed wars, economic crises, presidential infidelities and the Academy Awards. It brought his Gypsy father flying in from Italy in the company of the woman from *Elle*. Every network camera in the country was trained on the arrival gate at LAX when the father, as fashionably dressed as his son now that *Elle* had discovered him, stepped off the plane.

It was a short-lived pass through the limelight for the Gypsy, because Casanova Valentino Friedrich Don Juan Sabella didn't show, and no one's seen him since.

***

That was years ago, and in the world Cassy moved in, out of sight is as good as never having been there.

His name is never mentioned, except occasionally as the answer to a trivia question on a game show, or in a whisper now and then by lonely women in Los Angeles and Berlin, staring out a dark midnight window.

Ways to Save Money

Pinch pennies. Grow your own vegetables. Pull all your teeth with pliers and put the whole bloody mess under your pillow. Pretend you're asleep and when the tooth fairy shows up, wrestle her to the floor, tie and gag her, sell her to the sex trade.

Now we're talking big bucks. The tooth-fairy seed money will multiply like fishes and loaves, and soon you'll be a bona-fide Daddy Warbucks, selling arms under the table to everyone while your hands remain soft clean and pink. You can start your own mega-church and sleep with ex nuns and young boys. You can even buy back the tooth fairy for a night, her Tinker Bell magic diminished, but her legs still good.

Once you've reached this stage, everything you touch turns to gold. Even scandal can't hurt you, accusations roll off you like hot spit on a griddle. You're the talk of the town, a late-night-show sensation, the kind of hero that spawns fan clubs. Song writers write songs about you and you're made the ambassador to New Guinea. You're invited to witness lethal injections.

"Live simply so that I may simply live," are your parting words to the press as you board the plane to New Guinea, and the whole world tightens its belt.

Release Date

Sign here. Here's your watch and your compass. Your yo-yo and your skull ring. Your dogeared copy of *Walden Pond* and your little black book. Everything you came in with, just like it was when we stripped you and tossed you in the cold shower and powdered you down with lice killer. All except the little black book. The warden went through and lined out some names. You have no business associating with those people, not if you've been rehabilitated like you told the parole board. And you have, haven't you? Changed your ways?

He slipped on the ring and the watch. Stuffed *Walden* in his hip pocket. Disregarded the yo-yo and compass. Thumbed through the black book. The only names left were his mother and father and his retarded brother who was serving a different kind of sentence--life with no chance of parole on a funny farm. His mother and father had been dead for years.

He tried to remember the names of the women who'd been Xed out of the book. Tried to remember their touch and their faces. Not a one had paid him a visit. The rest of the names were political and drug related. And a Catholic priest who hid him out for a month before he decided to make a run for Mexico and got apprehended in Amarillo. That was thirty years back. The women who were still alive would be old and wrinkled. The priest defrocked. The drug connections OD'd or reformed by some Twelve-Step program. The politicians corrupt.

They threw back the bolt and the big gate swung open. He walked out, and the gate slammed shut behind him. He was 68 years old with $20 release money in his pocket, standing in the middle of a desert. A Greyhound came along and for $16.40 took him to the nearest town.

Begging Bowl

Imagine the surprise on his face when the pain let up.
Imagine his delight when the number ten kept appearing.
Imagine his confusion when the checks stopped coming and
they reclaimed the house. Imagine how sidetracked he got
thinking on the word "reclaim" when it was theirs all along,
just like the car and the wife who left when the checks stopped.

He thought about how the pain letting up tied in with the
number ten, and beyond that how both had nothing to do with
the house and the wife and the rest of it, but he drew blanks
when it came to conclusions. It was the brain damage, he'd
pieced that much together--his two-faced aunty when he was
a small child who was all smiles and honey around his parents
but a banshee when she had him alone, wrapping him naked
in duct tape, squeezing his little cock and balls while slamming
him alongside the head with a frying pan.

They concluded he was born that way but they worked
hard and got him smart enough to send to Iraq where a road
mine blew him out of his Hummer and gave him a walloping
concussion. And that's where the checks came from, from the
government.

Then they said he wasn't that bad off, he could get out there
and work like the rest of us. He couldn't of course, so there
he is at the age of 23, in line to get on a Greyhound to Florida
because he heard it was warm there, wearing strange clothes
and packing a begging bowl.

The other monks give him wide berth.

The Mongolian & the Mongoose

A Mongolian and a mongoose were matching wits on bar stools in a Saint-Lewis tavern; rolling dice with a dice cup for drinks. Putting quarters in the jukebox. Slow dancing off in the shadows.

The barkeep served them but he wasn't happy. Especially with the dancing. The men at the bar studied their drinks and showed nothing, but the barkeep knew a fight was coming. He glanced over at the Mongolian and the mongoose. The Mongolian was normal sized, but the mongoose was huge--on his hind legs dancing, he could lay his head on the Mongolian's shoulder, which he did.

The barkeep remembered reading somewhere that the mongoose is playful by nature, and swift. It can snatch up a cobra from behind its hood, sink in its teeth, and kill it just like that. But this particular mongoose, dancing on its hind legs, was awkward and kept stepping on the Mongolian's toes. The Mongolian didn't seem to notice, and he hadn't had that much to drink. He was in love, that's what it was. In love with a mongoose.

The tension was building in the men at the bar. It's a regular's bar, and strangers of any kind were not welcome, much less a Mongolian and a mongoose. And then there's the love thing, radiating out of them like cyanide fumes while they danced.

"Fuck this shit!" said Sweeny, the longshoreman. He kicked back his stool, and the other men at the bar did the same. They were ready to rumble.

The Mongolian and the mongoose disengaged. The mongoose went down on all fours and suddenly seemed dangerous, and the Mongolian unsheathed a long sword that somehow the barkeep had missed. He spun it over his head with alacrity before going into a battle stance, the sword extended in front of him, glinting in the pale light of the bar.

Keeping My Head Above Water

I'm trying to keep my head above water until help arrives--
a cruise ship, a submarine, a helicopter about to run out of gas.

I've thrown in the towel on my prayer beads. I'm back
to playing with cobras. A sharp rap on the upturned wicker
basket, take a deep breath and peek under. The snake only
strikes those who wish they were elsewhere.

Can you sense it, the stack of secrets I'm sitting on, like a
hen on raw oysters, like a Sumo wrestler on a 90-lb. weakling?
Mother Hubbard's children gone amok in a shoe.

Yes, yes, it's hereditary, passed along through the centuries
like hot stones, waiting for someone to do something original.

The last time I got more specific they shaved my head and
stuck electrodes in my eyeballs, so this will have to do until the
coast is clear.

Teddy Bears & Pandas

Most people care more for their teddy bear than a panda bear. Cute little thing with missing eyes, the root of all we believe in.

Swing me around daddy and drop me off in the briar patch. Somewhere in there there's a tar baby, icon of our comic-strip love. I want to smack it right in the face. Strike a blow for Jesus or some other mythical clown. One blow leads to another and soon we're covered with tar. This is how communities form. Brave new worlds. The story of Man begins. "Once upon a time in a far-away briar patch..."

This is not the hero's journey. This is the labyrinth without exit. This is the gnarly truth of a finger-snap lifespan. It gets censored out of the story, just like the panda bear.

It took a coy virgin to get the whole thing rolling. No wonder the Muslims are angry. They plant bombs in our teddy bears that we rock in our arms, hoping for sleep.

The clock ticks toward a mythological sunrise.

Writing His Memoirs

My father was a
misogynist
my mother the
Virgin Mary
my brother an
apologist for
war crimes
my twin sisters
born in formaldehyde
my first pet a
toad covered in
warts
that went **RIB-IT**
all night long
when the
moon was full.

Not an auspicious
family of origin
for a
would-be
Supreme Court Justice,
working nights
as a janitor
& drinking days
in obscure places,
groping thru a
correspondence-course

education
year after year
until his
hair turns gray.

Everyone's true
life story isn't
much different
from this.
The more successful
manage to
retire &
drive an RV
straight into
heart attack.

Madam Felicia

One random thought sparks another, and then the fun begins. A chain reaction of fractured thought. The split atom, infinitive, personality, loot from the audacious bank job in broad daylight.

All the way back to the Hole in the Wall Madam Felicia took us on one after the other in the back seat of the get-away. No need for Viagra for this crowd, no need of the soft-touch sex counselor, no problems getting it up. Jesus, the adrenalin rush when you come through the front door of the bank waving pistols and uzis and shooting out surveillance cameras is enough to drop a herd of elephants to its knees. And when the fool guard goes for his holstered revolver and you club him down--there's not a frigid woman lying face down on the floor who wouldn't spread her legs for you right there on the spot. And all the rest of it--bitch-slapping the desk jockey who tries to set off the silent alarm, comforting a small child who takes a shine to you, two men on look-out, one at the door, one up on a lobby counter grinning through his John-Travolta mask, Madam Felica in that tight black dress with the slit up the side, spiked heels, dark glasses, dark everything, deadpan and silent, smoking a Turkish cigarette in an ivory holder...the bitch is so cold she's hot, placing the plastic explosives in exactly the right spot on the vault door, a PhD in physics, years of working on the space shuttle, and then she'd had it.

Blam! The door blasts halfway across the vault ante-chamber and out in the bank women are screaming and the whole gang has erections and Sly Willie creams his britches like he does each and every time, which is why he gets last go at Madam Felicia in the back of the get-away, to give him time to recoup. The rest of us, we come like cannons the moment we slide it in, that's how hot we are.

Raking stacks of bills and jewelry into burlap bags, we leave looking like reproductions of Santa Claus--ho-ho-ho! Sometimes we take a hostage, always a woman, and have her go down on Madam Felicia, which they always do willingly, and the moment Madam Felicia cries out in ecstasy we toss the hostage bitch out of the car while two-wheeling around a curve and never look back. It's better than a coke high and lasts a little longer but the come-down is brutal. By nightfall we start drifting apart from each other.

Last night I went up to the ledge looking down on the lights of the city and there stood Madam Felica, smoking one of her Turkish cigarettes but without the holder. The holder is for show on the bank jobs. I went and stood beside her, and after awhile she held out her cigarette without looking at me and I took a drag and handed it back.

"One more job and I'm through," she said.

I didn't say anything. She said that after every job, it was part of how she unwound.

There isn't one of us who wouldn't lay his life down for Madam Felicia, even though we know that some day something in her will snap and she'll take us all out.

Terrible Tale of Woe

It's a terrible tale of woe they tell, old men with amputated limbs, limping home from a checkers game at the barber shop, flashing back to some scrap-heap war where white flags waved and bugles blew 24-7. The American Dream in tatters, tank tracks on the lawn, napalm lighting the night sky.

They have something new inside them that's filled the vacuum of lost hope, a ferocious mindset that protects a meager patch of turf.

This is what remains after the eradication of beauty.

The Skinny, the Poop

Here's the skinny, here's the poop, a microcosm of the Dilly Dally, spread in disarray on your kitchen table while you sleep, basking in moonlight under the gaze of a digital wall clock. A cornucopia of wrong answers, your life in a nutshell. And still when the alarm sounds you jump out of bed, touch your toes, say your prayers and brush your teeth, as if everything was on the up-and-up.

I've about had my fill--with monks and monkeyshines, peacocks and pheasants, the small rodents that dart through the juniper; with the wind-up toys of ambition, the sock full of laundromat quarters.

A hernia the size of a football, six Asian lovers and a cell phone--what's my problem? Someone's snapped off the aerial and side mirror on my car, that's what, the seat belt's broke and the driver's side door won't open. But I still get ten miles a gallon and have a loaf of stale bread in the cupboard.

I've got a picture album that goes back to childhood, and I've taken to cutting the faces off the old me and pasting them over the new, which can be taken two ways, depending on what you want out of life, depending on which way you're heading. The old me is the new me and the new me the old, and that pretty much sums things up and cancels out the whole show (because of rain, because of death, low attendance)...

The time for questions is past. They're out there in the dark shuffling the marquee letters like a jigsaw puzzle for the coming attraction.

I backflip out of orbit and tumble down like a snowflake.

You Take the High Road

Trying to map out a plan. Trying to rehash the obvious. Trying not to offend the rich Rajah with the 20" dick. I don't know where that came from, but there it is. Now I'll have to make my stand on the bonnie bonnie banks of Loch Lomand.

A song pops into my head. The trick is to keep it there, not blurt it out in this 6 a.m. restaurant. I'm the first customer through the door. Can you imagine the look on the waitress's face if all of a sudden I boom out, "Ye'll take the high road, and I'll take the low road, and I'll be in Scotland afore ye!" I can. I can imagine it well. I've seen it a thousand times before. It means trouble coming down the high road like an 18-wheeler with gun turrets. So I sit here minding my Ps and Qs and twiddle my thumbs. Rehash the obvious. Make a stab at a plan.

It takes its toll, surviving this long with your wits about you. It's like talking to a mirror, nothing resonates, nothing echoes. Now and then someone (a waitress, say, in a 6 a.m. restaurant) throws a look your way that if you didn't have your wits about you (*always,* rain or shine, peaking on acid, receiving your first holy communion, stroking your chin) you'd mistake for concern. But you know better, and any moment now she may make the dim connection, raise her arm slowly, index finger extended, and hiss like a body snatcher. Your best bet when you see that look is to smile, wave, maybe even wink, but don't, for the love of God, break out in song.

My worst fear and only hope is that some day someone's space rocket will dock with mine, and a strange misshapen sky pilot will hobble through the air lock.

Stay the Course

"Three birds in winter
flying in formation
melt into a *ménage a trois*."

Those are lines from a Pulitzer-nominated book of poems
by Gertrude the Turk, an until-recently much underrated and
even less known Greek poetess who once compared Rumi to
Kahlil Gibran on Radio Free Berlin.

Choosing Gertrude the Turk for a *nom de plume* might
explain her lack of popularity in her homeland, but how
account for her years of neglect world-wide? By way of
explanation, Gertrude cuts right to the chase--a conspiracy,
she says, fueled by vicious rumors spread by the Board
of Directors of The Gertrude Stein Adulation Society, a
nefarious, non-profit organization based in Philadelphia whose
CEO got waterboarded for funneling funds to a Lebanese
orphanage suspected of housing budding young terrorists--
three dunkings and he offered up Gertrude the Turk's name,
which led to her internment at Guantanamo.

Gertrude's getting locked down at Guantanamo triggered
a rash of academic interest in her work, but when an adjunct
professor of comparative literature at Wayne State University
got waterboarded for publishing a paper on her poetry,
comparing her with e.e. cummings, interest waned.

For her part, Gertrude went on a hunger strike and began
praying with the Muslims who constitute the majority of the
detainees at Guantanamo, which brought about a visit from a
delegation of Greek Orthodox priests who tried to talk some
sense into her head. The delegation stormed out after only a
few hours, flew back to Athens, and within a week Gertrude

the Turk's Greek citizenship was revoked, which started a chain reaction of happy coincidences.

For starters, Random House offered Gertrude a hefty advance for her autobiography, which prompted Ophra to read six poems by "G the Turk" (as the press was now calling her) on Ophra's trend-setting TV show. Leonard Cohen declared her the reincarnation of Gertrude Stein (raising the ire of the Gertrude Stein Adulation Society), and Rufus Wainwright wrote a song about her.

President George W. Bush, sensing an opportunity to pick up on some much needed good-guy PR, expressed the sentiment at a press conference that everyone should have a country and right there on the spot issued a pardon for the crimes Gertrude was suspected of committing, and--cutting through the red tape--declared her an American citizen by presidential decree. There was a ticker tape parade down Madison Avenue, and now GT (the latest press morph) is poet-in-residence at Yale University where her lectures are heavily attended.

Word has it that GT is hard at work on her autobiography, the publication of which is awaited with bated breath by bibliophiles the world over, except in Greece, where the book has been banned before it's been written.

All of which goes to prove that there's still hope for our troubled world if we're willing to put our noses to the grindstone and stay the course.

Crocodile Tears of an Iron-clad Mind

He laughs so hard he has tears in his eyes, but he's not
sorry, not amused. He's flinging articles of clothing this way
and that, a sock hanging from a low willow branch, his shorts
snagged in a plum tree. He's stark naked, the hounds tracking
a full wardrobe of false scents. The next thing is to jump in
the river and float downstream and not worry about climbing
out again until he gets there, wherever there is--a teeming
metropolis perhaps, like New Orleans.

This is how he's lived his life for so long he never thinks
about it until something punctures the membrane of his
thought.

Through that crude aperture he gets a glimpse of what he's
been running from and rushes in a state of hyper awareness to
mend the gash.

Not an Auspicious Time

I have a butterfly heart. A sapling of hope planted in concrete. A track record in love that boils down to a Wanted Poster. Dead or Alive with a preposterous reward.

These are not auspicious times. My best friends tie up the hot line with inside information on my whereabouts. My dossier grows fat as a mountain goat. My picture is showing up everywhere.

There must have been a point at which I could have stopped this from happening. If I'd only joined the Pied Piper when he charmed the children out of the safety zone. I could have led small parades with my twirling willow stick. Brought women happiness by telling them lies. Memorized the names of Hall of Fame indoctrinees and their long list of stats. Shunned drugs and alcohol and learned to start fires without matches. Been a clown or contender.

But I botched it.

We Do Our Work

The light's changed, the odds have doubled, mounds of pumpkins everywhere, sleigh bells not too far off, someone walks into my house and walks back out again with a Bi-Mart safety deposit box full of a poor man's dreams, and within a half hour after discovering it I'm up on a ladder wearing my dead father's Korean War wool-lined army cap with the big ear flaps, a cigarette dangling out of my mouth with a half inch of ash on it, wetting down high glass on this three-million dollar home, and on the other side of the glass is another world, a technicolor world with a roaring fire in a fireplace and two fat children maybe ten and twelve lounging in front of it, watching a TV over it about half as big as a movie screen, spooning down mounds of ice cream, registering me and not registering me simultaneously the way the rich do around "the help", they learn early and I can't help but see the similarity, the core sameness as the scene in *Sophie's Choice* that I watched for maybe the sixth time on DVD this past weekend where Sophie, emaciated and shorn and dressed in a gunny sack is marched through the mud of the Auschwitz concentration camp and through a crude wooden door with coils of barbwire over it into the technicolor world of the camp commander, Rudolph Hoess, a lush garden with the Hoess children frolicking in it, into the small mansion of a house where Hoess' wife has pies baking in the oven, into the basement where she is showered and deloused and given a clean gunny sack to wear, up into Hoess' office where he paces furiously and gives rapid dictation that even in her degraded condition Sophie takes down to perfection in a language that is not hers.

A phone call telling me my granddaughter has been busted for pot possession in Kentucky rounds off this fine day, and the first scent of snow blows in on a brisk mountain wind.

Advice on How to Get Right with the World

Advice comes winging in out of left field, like a canary in a mine shaft, l ike a parrot down on its luck: stop saying what you're saying and say what people want you to say and say hey! -- you'll go straight to the top. You'll reap benefits. Big bucks, hot chicks, a tiny corner in a right-wing time capsule. Blast off, and there goes your digital voice, mumbling platitudes to future multitudes on a far-away planet. You're an earth version of Superman.

Here's the gist of your problem: you turn the host back into bread. Take a hard look at your motives. There they are, shielding their eyes from the searchlight, lined up like suspects against the north face of childhood.

A Life Well-Spent

I've spent the last third of my life exploring new terrain and wound up right back where I started. Something was set in stone the moment my mother slapped my tiny hands away when I reached for her breast in my birthing bed.

This could be fantasy, this could be truth. It could be both and probably is. There is a direct link between plastic bottles with rubber nipples and the banking system; between political rigmarole and modern warfare; between the music industry and genocide. Don't take my word for it, look into your heart. What is that off in the tom-tom shadows, crouched and sucking its thumb? Now you've done it. It will take a cornucopia of pharmaceuticals to blot out this grisly vision.

"Level out!" ground control radioed the test pilot who was rocketing straight into the stratosphere, and he yanked off his oxygen mask and kept right on climbing.

Agility

It's unwise to
knock me
off balance.

I spring back
with alacrity.

Bluntness

People who
drink like
I did &
never get
depressed
are stupid.

Strength

Having your
deepest privacy
violated
is the
only way to
become strong.

Precision

Precision is
required when
operating on
someone's heart
unless you're
really not
trying to
save them.

Waiting for Paul Bowles

Carry me to a
far-away place.
Let's pretend
I have a
passport & a
will to live.
Drop me off
at an
outdoor cafe
in Tangiers.
I'll stay there
until closing,
waiting on
Paul Bowles.

Disregard
rumors
of his death.

Point Man for Spontaneity

Even when it's your birthday and you walk into a dark house and all the lights come on and sixteen naked women burst out of sixteen gigantic multi-layered cakes like sperm whales and a roomful of properly attired people wearing party hats yell Happy Birthday! simultaneously and begin shaking rattles and blowing horns, even then planning has no part in the rapid-fire combat in your convoluted brain.

Instead of being rocked back on your heels, you say something highly inappropriate and unexpected, laugh uproariously and begin stripping off your clothes and lunging after naked woman smeared with chocolate icing who squeal and scatter, creating alarming unexpected naked pandemonium.

You pin a cake woman to the wall in the hallway and begin licking icing from her taut nipples. She throws her head back and laughs and runs her hands through your hair, and the other fifteen gather round, arching their backs and cupping their breasts, and you drop down on your knees.

Guests are bunched up at the entrance to the hallway, and your wife, who thought to show you just how spontaneous she can be with this little birthday surprise, barks, "Carl! For Christ *sake!"*

Sensing the flow going out of things, you toss a naked woman over your shoulder and march off for the bedroom.

***

By the time you come back out, everyone has left. The naked woman grabs her clothes that are neatly folded on a chair, dresses and leaves too.

Your wife is sitting at the kitchen table in her seductive dress that she bought on impulse that very afternoon, her party hat still perched on her head. She's staring at her hands on the table top.

"We need to talk," she says, without looking up.

You bend and drink straight from the tap at the kitchen sink. and without saying anything, walk out the front door, not bothering to put on the clothes that make you invisible.

Paranoia

The paranoid
are guilty
whether they've
done anything
or not.

Stormy Dark Beauty

There's a
stormy dark
beauty I
see almost
daily who
when she
meets my eyes
looks away
& then
back again,
smiling faintly.

She has
no defense
against
what I
see in her.

The Kill

Life has
driven me
back into
short poems of
brief observations.

It pauses to
catch its
breath &
wipe the
sweat from
its brow
& then
moves in
for the kill.

Passing Muster

Somewhere in
early childhood
a deep understanding
rose up in me
which made it
impossible to
pass the
first grade.

Smoke & Mirrors

The world is
going to hell
in a
hand basket &
people sneer
at me
for smoking
like somehow
I'm to
blame.

Rance

Rance came out of a hard nap to a ringing phone. It's a woman who is so much like a girl, saying in her usual highly-intelligent state of heart-stealing confusion that never fails to cast a spell over him, something about missed phone calls and a supper invitation.

After he hangs up, in the middle of a piss, he experiences an explosion of post-nap anger, and what does that say about our boy Rance? What *is* Rance, what makes his clock tick as he flies out the door caught up in an ongoing swarm of both sequential and random synapses, starts the car and drives off?

Even before he pulls from the curb a synapse triggers a Voice that says, "Rance, baby, you've got to keep this kind of stuff under wraps, you can't be blabbing it out to the world-at-large, it's singing to the tone deaf, and that's why they come back at you so hard, label what you say ugly, they can't *hear it* so they make up what they think it is and one of these days they're going to nail you to a cross, baby, and--*oh no!* Rance, damn your eyes! *Don't you do it!* Don't tell them about *me!*"

Gliding through a stop sign, Rance wonders what it means if his own Voices turn on him. Just how far gone does that make him?

He passes an afternoon movie theater, and queued halfway down the block are kids ages 7 to 14, sitting some of them in deck chairs, others leaning against the brick wall, some actually lying on air mattresses. They're not talking and they're not smiling, they're waiting for the matinée opening of the new *Harry Potter* movie, and there's someone who knew to keep her mouth shut about the Voices, J.K. Rowling. "If," says a Voice in his head, "she even *has* Voices. If any of these wall-eyed children do. Maybe the whole world is brain damaged ..."

About then the black schizophrenic in rags who wanders the town shows up across the street from the queued children, laughing gleefully and doing a little jig and pointing at them with an extended arm. Then he sees Rance drive by and the laughter fades, his arm falls slowly to his side, and he follows the car down the block with his eyes--Rance can see him in the side-view mirror.

An image rises up in Rance's mind of a high city ledge lined with cooing pigeons that suddenly explode into the air in a wild tangle of flapping wings...

Space Travel

I travel in &
out of space.
I'm not the
only one.
I see nephews &
nieces out there,
rummaging thru
bins of used days.
I saw you once,
primping in front of a
looking glass.
I cleared my throat
the way I used to
when you
took my breath away,
but you paid me
no mind.

"Are you listening
to me?"
someone on the
other side of the
table asks.

I drop a
sugar lump
into my coffee &
stir it.

"Yes," I say.
"Please go on."

The Treasure Chest of Childhood

He pried the
lock off the
treasure chest &
out spilled
bronze pennies &
mildewed enigmas.
Four wooden
soldiers &
six cash-back
dilemmas.
A tiny tickle &
an innocent smile.
A currency that
drove him
straight into
bankruptcy.

When he
tried to
jam it
all back
in again
it wouldn't
fit.

Inflation,
he thought,
& then
tied off
for his
last fix
before they
sent him to
treatment.

Believing in Shit

He carries a
pistol with a
single bullet
in it.

When people
come on strong
about shit they
claim to
believe in,
he whips out
the pistol,
twirls the cylinder,
puts the barrel
to his head
& pulls the
trigger.

Then he hands
the pistol
to them.

"Here,"
he says.
"Your turn."

And Baby Makes Three

There's a plot afoot against childhood deformity. In summer it upgrades into a conspiracy. But its intentions are good. Its intentions are to blot out unpleasantness, arch enemy of the cushy life. It's been building incrementally for some time now, and it's well disguised as something else.

For example, right in this 88 Chevy Caprice, the back windows roll down only halfway, ostensibly to keep small children from toppling out while roaring down the freeway doing 80. But truth is, the idea is to keep the children from *climbing* out or being *yanked* out if the car is on fire and the doors are stuck. If they climb out, they might live, burn-scarred and hideous, wandering the halls of our public schools, showing up in darkened movie theaters and at 4th of July parades.

And then there are the air bags. A head-on collision can cause as much disfiguration in a child as a fire, so out pop the air bags and smother them.

Of course disfigurement in death is also unpleasant, which is why we have the closed-casket funeral, which is a thing of beauty as well as an economic enhancer: a closed $10,000 coffin in a sea of red roses, organ music wafting softly through the dimly lit funeral parlor, which--doing its part to stamp out unpleasant terminology--is now more often called a Tribute Center.

The helmet law for kids riding bikes is more subtle. It's not brain injury that's of primary concern but hair loss due to scalp damage that might result in hair growing back in patches, an unpleasant thing to behold down the line, in--for instance--someone flipping your burger at McDonald's or trying to sell you a house in the trouble-free suburbs.

Simply sharing this information with you gives rise to unpleasantness, and I apologize. But there's a bright star on the evening horizon--Disney has come to the rescue with a win-win solution. Using its reputation for blotting out unpleasantness wherever it shows its disfigured face, and employing a small army of lobbyists and throwing open a Pandora's Box of Pay-o-la, Disney has come up with a plan that once it is implemented into national legislation will require every child who fits the new law's description of deformity to--whenever the child is outside the confines of the home or there are visitors in the home--wear one of numerous full-body Disney suits,depending on the child's temperament and sex and the nature of the deformity, including: Mickey Mouse, Minnie Mouse, Donald Duck, Daisy Duck, April Duck, Pluto, Baby Red Bird, Bambi, Big Al, Big Mamma, Doofus Drake, Goofy, Cinderella and all of the Seven Dwarfs.

Once the new law goes into effect, air bags and restricted back-seat windows and helmets will become a thing of the past. In time disfigured children encased in full-body Disney suits will outnumber normal children. In time they will bond with their character, and Disney Suit stores will spring up to accommodate the children with larger suits as they grow into adulthood. Eventually, not wanting their children to stand out, to be, as it were, freaks, parents of normal children will begin encasing them in Disney suits, too.

This is the wave of the future. The day will come when every country we conquer will be occupied by an army of Mickey Mouses, and the world will finally see the futility of resisting our domination.

Life is Like a
Crystal Ball

Life is like a
crystal ball.
Or Hamlet's
skull.
Or one of
those snow
globes
full of
liquid
with a
plastic cabin
glued inside.
Shake it
twice,
a winter
wonderland.

Things never
look the same
for long.
From year to year,
day to day,
minute to minute.
Lovers comes & go,
dogs die.
You're yanked out of
one mind set &
slammed down in another.
You drink coffee black &
then with cream
& then not at all.
You drink alcohol
with a vengeance &

think you'll
never quit but
25 years
down the line
you do.

In the course
of a day
you wake up
happy &
go to bed blue,
feel young again
& sadly old,
see universal
truth &
stand bewildered
at a crosswalk;
feel tenderness
for all mankind &
shut off from
the world.

Thru it all
you're certain
that you'll
live forever
& then one day
you're not so sure.

Life Passes You By

The Age of Reason. The Iron Age. The iron horse. The steel trap. The better mouse trap. Cunnilingus in a sausage factory. Fellatio in the Eiffel Tower. Clever people put their heads together and out pops a euphemism. A virgin birth, first step toward a rosy crucifixion. There must be some way out of here without being turned into Plastic Man or the Incredible Hulk.

Pop culture, popcorn, soda pop and a double-feature matinée. It's dark when you get outside again, and you can't find your car. You jangle your keys in your pocket and whistle. Maybe it will come like a dog.

Come like a dog! Flashbacks to the sausage factory and the Eiffel Tower. Bad dog! Heel!

People give you a wide berth, get in their own cars and drive off. The parking lot is empty.

You don't even report the thing stolen. You walk all the way home and go in through the back door. Inside in the dark there's a cuckoo bird blapping off the windows and ceiling. You chase it around with a spatula, but it's too quick for you. You settle down over yesterday's mail and rip open the top envelope. Read it by candlelight.

A Norwegian girl who a long time ago took you to Valhalla and back has settled in Paris where spring has erupted in cherry blossoms and daffodils. She's just spent the whole afternoon at an outdoor cafe drinking espresso with a German.

The candle blows out in a back draft, and you realize that your life has passed you by.

Estranged from the Sun

He stared at his reflection in the kitchen window and then belched. He walked out of the kitchen, hitting the light switch as he entered the living room.

He sat down on the couch and made doodles on a napkin with a ballpoint pen until the napkin was full. He crumpled the napkin and flicked it. It lay on the living room rug, slowly unfolding, as if it were cellophane.

He felt like he should stand up and he felt like he should remain sitting. He felt equally strong about both options. He realized these weren't really options, but this didn't change the way he felt. He felt he should do something, but he knew it made no difference to him or anyone else whether he did something or not. Still, he felt this way.

There was one person left in the world who when he was in her company made him feel that their lives mingled. He knew from experience that this was an illusion, but it is the only illusion that makes life bearable. Knowing this took something away from it, but it was still there, which says something for its power.

Every morning for a long time now he wakes up with the sensation of being crushed or strangled. It is his own mind causing these sensations. A part of him wants it to happen. A part feels that this is the only thing left that has meaning. His dreams confirm this.

He stood up from the couch and stared at the napkin. It had ceased unfolding. It had gone as far as it could in its effort to regain its original shape. He nudged the napkin with the toe of his shoe. No response.

The doors were locked and the porch light was on. There was nothing left to do.

Inherit the Wind

When they refuse you
everything &
still you
keep coming,
that's when they
bolt upright
in bed screaming
Mama!

They peek thru
the curtains &
the street is
teeming with
monsters
no bigger than
hedgehogs,
prancing in moonlight
as if they might
inherit the wind.

Well Informed

Some people
need to be kept
well-informed.
About the weather,
dead celebrities,
exploding economies.
They're riddled with
anxiety--
about failure,
about success,
about their
sex lives &
their children.
About the
nameless dread,
which is what anxiety
boils down to.
Anxiety about
anxiety then,
a delicious black angst.
The thing gets
compounded until they're
lashing out
at each other
with laptops &
cell phones &
turning up
cum laude
on arrival,
murmuring *mea culpa*
in their
drug-infested sleep,

sliding down a
steep scree of
mucus into a
dark moonless night.

We are being consumed
by a ferocious
momentum.

Sticks & Stones

I had a talking stick that appeared in a recurring dream, and at the age of five it materialized at the foot of my bed. An ordinary stick, except it could talk.

"Pick me up," it said, "and use me to draw a circle around you in the sand of your pain. Then make a line inside the circle. Now sit down in the circle with your legs crossed and close your eyes. This is how I'll take you through life. There will be those who will enter the circle with war clubs, but no one will cross the line. Do you get my drift?"

Of course I didn't. I was only five. But it was the first time I'd ever felt recognized, so I did it.

It was many years before the stick spoke again. "Are you awake?" it said.

"Yes," I said.

"Good," said the stick. "Now open your eyes and step out of the circle. There are stones to turn over."

I used the stick to turn over the stones, and out would spring coral snakes and scorpions. I'd twirl the coral snakes in the air with the stick until they grew dizzy, and then I'd lay them gently back down and say, "There now." The scorpions were a different matter. They'd try to dart up my pants leg and I'd have to step on them. It never made me feel good, stepping on the scorpions, but the stick would sing lullabies as we lay under the stars at night, and that helped some. Nevertheless, my eyes grew sad.

And then came the dark holes. I noticed that people who railed against me for turning over stones, when they thought no one was watching, would stick their hands in dark holes. Their eyes would glaze over with pleasure, and they'd moan. After some time it was all I could think about. I wanted to do it too. I took to leaving the stick out of earshot when I slept, and then one day I did it.

There was something warm and fuzzy inside the hole. It sucked my fingers and sent sensual waves through my body. When I finally broke free, I felt something was missing in my life. I stopped turning over stones and had a hard time sleeping.

And then one night as I lay under the stars tossing and turning, the stick appeared and began beating me mercilessly. "Shame!" said the stick. "Shame!"

For thirty days the stick held me under its spell without food or drink. During this time I had visions, and it was revealed to me that the warm fuzzy things in the holes were nocturnal. They came out at night and ravaged children. By sunrise they were gone again, waiting in their holes for someone to stick his hand in.

The stick drew a new circle around me. It was much larger, and more a trench than a circle. There was no longer need of a line.

"These are my last words," said the stick, "and then I must leave you. Listen well:

"Under stones you'll find labels like kike, nigger and wop. In the black holes are defoliation and ethnic cleansing. One group sounds worse than it is. The other is worse than it sounds. Now go forth." And with that the stick vanished.

I wrote these strange events down as a children's story and called it *Sticks and Stones,* but no one would publish it.

The Bust

They dragged him out by his heels before dawn and slapped him into the wall. They read him his rights and then clubbed him senseless. They tossed him into the paddy and raced off thru the night.

The neighbors stood on their lawns in their jammies and watched the whole thing go down. They looked at each other across the green grass, nodded and then looked away. They went slow as molasses back into their houses, back to bed and their bright dreamless sleep.

They woke up the next morning and stepped into the shower. Some sang, some hummed, some slumped under the torrent until the water ran cold. They all sat down to breakfast. They all ate the same thing--white toast with one butter pad, black coffee and a small piece of fruit. Then they stepped out the door in their outfits and backed out of the driveway.

Somewhere in the gridlock, they turn on their radios. A familiar voice is waiting for them. "Good morning!" it says, and they smile. "Did we sleep well?" They nod. "Did we dream?" They nod again. Yes they did, they dreamed the same dream, a man screaming and kicking was carted off by police. They woke up safe in their beds. Grateful and well-rested, they got up and commenced.

They're feeling good now, ready for work. The radio bursts out in song and they all sing along, even the ones who slumped in the shower.

Someone is taking very good care of them. Someone is making sure they're not harmed. Their only fear is that they might become the man in the dream. But this shouldn't happen if they keep up the good work. They avert their eyes from the rearview mirror and drive on down the freeway.

He Covered the Waterfront

With a ball-peen hammer he'd tap messages on ribbed metal conduits three feet in diameter that ran along the train tracks and down into the harbor, then cup his ear and listen to the echoed moans within. He did it only during daylight hours for fear of breaking someone's heart.

He slept nights under a viaduct in a burnt-out Olds-88 with the doors, hood and wheels gone. He had the back seat and a Chinese dwarf dressed in burlap had the front. On cold nights the dwarf would climb into the back and spoon against him for warmth. There was nothing sexual about it, but it filled them both with tenderness.

His family knew where he was but pretended not to. It was easier that way. His mother packed a lot of guilt--she should have put a stop to it when he was just a small boy and started bringing wounded bird's home to heal. From there it went to stray dogs and cats and then human beings with crazed eyes. If only they'd put him on medication, maybe none of this would have happened.

It surprised them when he signed up for the army. But then he learned Arabic and went AWOL and gave all his money to children in villages he passed through--that's how they tracked him down. Six months in Guantanamo and a full year on a nut ward and he wound up on the waterfront.

A cub reporter got wind of what was going on and did a human interest story for the local paper, but his father had connections and killed it before it went to press.

It was election year, and their one big hope was that maybe Obama would get elected and put a stop to such things.

A Girl Named Cheating

The bear went over the mountain, and what do you think he saw? Another landscape of burning bushes between him and the next mountain.

The bear's name was Syphilis. He got it from a Greek he ate. Once you wander into the flaming wilderness in quest of vision, nationalities fall away and you're fair game for anything. It beats cheating.

***

I once knew a girl named Cheating. She'd eat Greeks by the truckload and whoever else wandered in. She had a shack with a red porch light on the edge of base camp and a sixth sense that told her these boys on their way up the mountain longed for one last taste of what they were about to give up. There's a fortune to be made on the dark side of virtue.

Cheating worked the trade for longer than time can measure, and then she packed up and went back to the city, following advice Mose Allison had given her years earlier when he blew into base camp to play a gig. "If you're goin' to the city," Mose said, "you better bring some cash. Because the people in the city, don't mess around with trash." Well, she'd left the city broke and now she was returning with her pockets lined with gold. Cheating bought a nice place on Russian Hill and fed the parrots that filled the San Francisco sky like green bats. People called her Madam.

Night after night Cheating's lawn became a vigil of candle-holding fools. And then one night the front door opened, and there she stood in all her splendor with her black bear on a leash. The crowd began to chant, softly at first, but building: "Cheating, Cheating, Cheating, *Cheating!*"

Cheating waiting until the chant reached fever pitch, and then she yanked her bear inside and slammed the door shut.

Crossing Over

When I met her
she rode a bike
with one pedal
& hadn't yet
turned twenty.

We lived together
six years & then
she went to college
& left me for
a boy who
studied Latin.

The last I heard
she had a
PhD, a baby
& was married
to a physicist
from the Ukraine.

The boy who
studied Latin
has returned to
live with his parents,
& I've crossed a line
where I'm
more one with
the night sky
than the
life I've led.

Crazy John Bennett

Back in the
day I was
known by a
certain bar crowd
as
crazy John Bennett.
I would
walk into the
Corner Stone Tavern
on a
quiet afternoon &
a cheer would
go up from
the regulars.
They knew that
before the
night was over
I'd be
biting the
heads off
chickens.

I tried
changing my name
to Jabony Welter,
but things
stayed
pretty much
the same.

Salesmanship

Stepping into
the local
music shop
to buy an amp
I plug the thing in
& try playing
Summer Time
but the owner is
three stalls down
playing blues
on his guitar &
I can't
break into
Summer Time
to save my life.
Instead I
get my harp
behind his
guitar.

When the song's
over he
sticks his
head around
the corner.
"So whatcha think?"
he says

"I'll take it,"
I say.

A Million Words

There are a million words in the English language. A third of them have to do with losing weight and coveting your neighbor's wife. Another third have to do with exorcism and circumcised goats. The rest are divided evenly between science, art and codependency.

Compare this with Spanish where 60% of the words have to do with spicy food and male supremacy. Or Russian where each and every word is in some way tied in with tanks, executions and potato famine. Or Gaelic where the whole language is drunk on whiskey. Or an obscure Amazonian jungle dialect consisting of nothing but tongue clicks.

There've been studies made, but the whole world still waits for some anthropologist with the aid of six chimps and a coral snake to sum up just what it is we've been trying so long to say.

FOOTBALL PLAYER WITH HEAD INJURY DEVELOPS A MENTAL ILLNESS WHERE HE CAN'T STOP ASKING SEXUAL QUESTIONS

"How'd you like to spoon up to Reece Witherspoon on a water bed? How'd you like to fill a spoon with crystal and watch her take it up her nose? How'd you like to go on a blind date with Nicole Kidman and out of nowhere say, "I want to fuck you in your little-girl bed cluttered with dolls and teddy bears," and then before she can recover from her astonishment say, "Just kidding!" and see if she gets the joke? How'd you like to ask Catherine Zeta-Jones how is it such a dark-skinned beauty comes from Scotland? How'd you like to exhume Marilyn Monroe's remains and make a fortune selling crack pipes made from her bones? How'd you like to slam Katharine Hepburn up against a wall and tell her you're twice the man Spencer Tracy was? How'd you like to take Angelina Jolie roller skating in Mexico City? How'd you like to take Audrey Hepburn to breakfast at Tiffany's? How'd you like to father six kids with the fat lady in the circus? Any old circus. Any old fat lady. How'd you like to have sex with Mother Teresa and cause her to renounce her vows? How'd you like to give mouth-to-mouth to Princess Di after the car wreck and take her last breath into your lungs? How'd you like to return a kick off from the Los Angeles Lakers for a touchdown? How'd you--"

"Hold on a minute now!" says his shrink. "A kick off from the *Lakers?*"

"How about a team of Amazon Lesbians?" says the once-famous linebacker.

"That's more like it," says the shrink. "Now we're getting someplace..."

The Word Forever

People who use
the word forever
need their
heads examined.
I had mine
examined &
they prescribed
a trip to
Asia in a
silk shirt &
patten-leather shoes.
When I asked about
the plane fare
they smiled &
said that's
not included.
Uh-huh I said &
they said
you'd better
think about your
future.
Right then &
there I
knew I'd
walked into a
trap.
Bamboo shoots
sprang up
around me &
somewhere far away
a baboon howled.

You talked
your way

into this
I said to myself,
let's see you
talk your
way out.
I produced my
credit card
that I'd been
meaning to
shred &
the bamboo shoots
retracted.
The baboon's
howl became
a purr, &
dressed in
silk shirt &
patten-leather shoes,
I left without meeting
anybody's eyes,
a one-way
ticket to Asia
in my
unwashed hand.

Stars Fell on Alabama

Stars fell on Alabama
& people who hadn't
been out of bed
in weeks because of
acute depression
made their way
on trembling legs
to pull back the curtain &
stare in amazement.
In Birmingham traffic
(light as it was at that hour)
came to a standstill &
the countryside
outside the cities
pulsed with pools of
blue light.

It wasn't like
the scientists had
told them.
Stars weren't
gigantic balls of fire
like the sun,
they were flat &
shaped like the
star on top of the
Christmas tree,
like the stars we
all drew in kindergarten
when the teacher said,
"Draw me a sky picture."

They were no more than
three feet in circumference,

some of them lying
flat on the ground
some caught in the
branches of trees
some with one of their
points embedded in
the earth.

At first people
stood in awe &
just stared,
but gradually they
began moving in close &
the bravest among them
reached out &
touched them.
They were cool
to the touch,
smooth & lighter
than they looked.
People began
picking them up &
holding them close
like babies,
laughing softly &
shaking their heads.
There were
millions of them,
but by sunrise they'd
all been gathered &
stored in
basements & attics.

The next morning
was like any other,
except no one

turned on their radios
or televisions &
everyone walked
to where they were going.
Up in space
a spy satellite
picked up a
warning signal &
trained its cameras &
listening devices
on Alabama,
holding them there
until disappearing
around the earth's
curvature.

What the satellite
sent back to earth
translated into
soft lilting melody,
& at CIA headquarters
in Langley,
people drifted into
the parking lots &
looked skyward,
a hand held to their eyes.

The Color of Equality

White men, red men, black men, yellow men and green men from Mars, circling for landing clearance.

"Tower to alien craft, you're cleared for a holding pattern at 5000 feet, repeat, 5000 feet. Meanwhile, beam down Scotty, we know he's up there. We need a little face time. Do you read me?"

"Hrompa gak kot koot kawanga raqnaptaw koowee!"

They ran that through the decoder and came up empty handed, and then they made a voice pattern copy and slapped it down on the desk of the Pennsylvania Polyglot, a guy who sat around all day doing nothing but picking zits and whose job description was conjured out of thin air by his uncle, a powerful flight-attendant lobbyist.

"We need a translation pronto," said the shift supervisor, "or we'll have to send up the fighter jets and blow those creeps out of the sky, Scotty with them."

A half hour later the Pennsylvania Polyglot strolled into the bee hive of the flight tower and announced rather drolly that Scotty was in the men's room of the space craft and refused to come out, and the green men from Mars were going to circle the earth three times and if we didn't have our shit together to give them a landing clearance by then, they were going to turn everyone on earth green and fly home again.

This is usually where the hot line to the president gets activated, but the shift supervisor hesitated. How would a black president take the news that aliens were going to turn him green?

The air traffic controllers, totally whacked out on crystal meth and bouncing in their chairs like syphilitic monkeys, joyfully began shooing planes from the D.C. sky like flies, redirecting them to New York and Newark, Detroit and Atlanta and St. Paul, clearing the deck for action.

The aliens completed their three laps and then banked hard and began radiating waves of equality over the entire planet, turning everyone green.

A green President Obama went on world-wide television and urged everyone to remain calm, and Fox News interrupted his broadcast to have a green Rush Limbaugh deliver a scathing, off-the-cuff speech in which he denounced the Green Scare as something Obama himself had orchestrated to deflect attention from his plot to destroy unborn children and euthenize old folks, thereby showing his true colors, which were all yellow.

Millions the world over took to the streets chanting in many languages, "You lie! You lie!" and Obama flew off to Camp David in Air Force One where he brooded in seclusion for forty days and nights and then resigned the Presidency.

Everyone moved up a notch, and by the time Christmas rolled around, department stores were reporting record sales. A Gallop poll showed that nine out of ten adult Americans believed the Green Scare was a gigantic hoax and that we had been green all along.

After that new wars broke out in Iran and Turkey, and things went back to normal.

Scotty was never heard from again, and he was skillfully erased from all Star Trek reruns.

Taps

He blew the bugle
at 4 a.m.
for the
company to
fall out in
formation
because his
days were
growing short &
he wanted to
march his men
down the
back alley
of time
for all the
world to see.

But no more than
thirty men
came out
of the barracks,
half of them
still in
pajamas &
slippers &
only three
carrying rifles.

His life's
soldiers were
reluctant to
gather all in
one place.
They'd never

done it before
so why now?
They were
specialists
in cognito,
they liked to
infiltrate &
play possum &
when the time was right
torch the city
steal the silver
& run.
The only time
they ever did
real fighting
was when
they were
backed into a
corner.
Then they were
as ferocious as
Greeks.
How many times
had the
enemy wheeled a
Trojan Horse
up to the gate &
they set it
on fire with arrows?
How many times
had they
slipped through the
ranks of some
golden-haired Custer
like Ninjas?
They held things

for ransom
no one knew
they were missing.
They reenlisted
time &
again to
carry his
sorry ass
through to the
armistice.
& now that they
were finally there
he wants them to
go on parade.

Choked with emotion
he blows the
bugle again,
blows it
like Gabriel
like Miles Davis
like Chet Baker,
& the troops
still inside
lean out the
windows &
listen.

Imaginary Phone Calls

I make imaginary phone calls.
Sometims I call the Pope of Rome.
It's good between us,
because we both speak German.
He has a private line.

I don't understand his thing for
young boys or his Nazi past,
but when he breaks down & cries,
my heart goes out to him.
I'm a sucker for tears.

I'm still a sucker for the beauty of
young women, too. I mean,
it stops me dead in my tracks.
It's not lust. I begin to
realize this as
lust wanes. I think most men
have this until the day they die.
The Pope says he knows where
I'm coming from, but I
don't trust the Pope
in such matters.

Sometimes I call Studs Terkel.
Studs tells me to get my
head out of my ass.
Crocodile tears, says Studs.
Even psychopaths cry.

I suppose I trust Studs
more than the Pope,
but my heart doesn't
reach out to him.

I sometimes wonder
why that is,
but I know I'll
never find out.
Studs ain't Woody Gutherie,
the answer lies
in there somewhere.

Quite often the number I dial
is busy. This makes me uneasy.
Who could they be talking to?

I came this close to
swimming into an ocean of
acceptance recently, but
the tide changed &
washed me ashore.
There I lay among the
sand dollars & seaweed,
gasping like a fish
out of water.
There was a tendency toward
panic, but then I realized
this is where Man
first grew legs.

I took out my cell phone &
punched in God's number.
I had no idea what I'd say
when He answered.

The Down Side of Solitude

Not to be a
crybaby but
I need
an agent
a secretary
a live-in
file clerk who
can also cook &
give back rubs
someone with a
wide streak of
devotion to
save me from
myself to
scoop up this
avalanche of
words &
shape it
form it
get it
out there
someone to
make contacts
someone
charming who
can sell
do lunches
make phone calls
fly off for some
face time
sign on the
dotted line.

I need a

Maxwell Perkins
or a
John Martin to
bridge the gap
between the
stormy tundra I
wander &
wherever it is
the rest of you
live.

I'm being
devoured by
my own
imagination.

Health Care

Pearls and girls, the spoils of war and romance, if it rhymes and has rhythm, use it to pry the lid off secrecy, like a kitchen knife under the lid of a jar of peaches. Is the hiss the sound of air escaping or entering the jar?

Don't answer questions like that, don't elaborate as Lyndon Johnson liked to say, push on now that you've got the upper hand, this is the road to absolution.

I see my V.A. care provider once a year and we talk books, war and women, philosophy, street drugs and endurance. When I first went in there seven years ago to claim my benefits he spotted me on the weigh-in scale where I was delivering a monologue of one-liners to a pale-green stucco wall not six inches from my nose--"He's mine," he said in passing, and snatched my folder from the in-take nurse.

He was 35 then, five years as a Green Beret under his belt, made his way up from a Texas white-trash trailer park, *cum laude* in pre-med, a black belt in karate, a lean, mean, hungry machine.

As the years went by I watched him enter middle age and his brazen certainty give way to thoughtful pauses. He listens now like he didn't at the onstart, and he's beginning to see in me what he only sensed with a sterling savage instinct the day he snatched me off the scale. In our annual one-hour sessions we manipulate our differences like clay into the shape of what it is we have in common.

Today I gave him what he needed to hear to carry on through the next twenty years, and he was so thankful he forgot to even take my pulse.

It Will Be There When the Oil Runs Out

I met up with some Gypsies in Brussels forty years ago. Grant and I had just backpacked in from Luxembourg, flat-broke. We went into this Bohemian/workers' bar in the street-action part of town (a sprawling place with an elevated section almost like a stage) and ordered two beers we couldn't pay for. It was one of those mini moments of truth.

And then the Gypsies (there was a long table of them dominating the elevated section of the bar) began playing guitars and shaking tambourines and singing Flamenco while a beautiful young woman danced; afterward she made the rounds with an upturned hat.

I looked at Grant and Grant looked at me and then I pulled out my harmonica and began playing Bob Dylan songs while Grant (eyes closed, head back, and on his feet now) began to sing. "The answer my friend, is blowing in the wind," Grant sang, and when he was done he marched straight up to the Gypsy's table, took off his Greek fisherman's hat, turned it upside down, and held it out.

The Gypsies stared at him in stone-cold silence for what seemed like a very long time, the whole bar was watching, and then an old Gypsy with a face like seasoned leather scooped a handful of change out of the dancing girl's collection basket and poured the coins into Grant's hat. The table exploded in laughter, some gajos at the bar actually clapped, and when the night was over the Gypsies took us with them to where they lived on the top floor of a condemned boarded-up building in a section of Brussels that was nothing but boarded-up buildings.

We sat around by candlelight drinking wine and smoking

hashish and the Gypsies mapped out their strategy for the day to come. In the morning they sent us on our way with enough folding money to get us to Munich.

This is the human spirit that the less you understand it and the more you persecute it, the more it eats your guts out. It will be there when the oil runs out.

Blood of the Savior

My feet are baking in my shoes. I should take them off, the shoes. I should get out of this furnace of a car and walk over to the island of grass. I should take off my shirt, too. Lie on my back on the grass and make whatever noises come out of my mouth straight into the sky. I should tear these ties that bind from me and hold them over my head in clenched fists.

My mind waves aren't waves. They're a tumble of right angles with razor-sharp edges. They lacerate. My brain is a hemorrhage. "Stop the bleeding!" the corpsman barked out in special-ops training, and I laughed and laughed and couldn't stop until finally they yanked me out of there.

A lieutenant sat me down in his office and called me son. I started laughing again. The right angles tumbled and welled. My eyes were blood-shot, the tips of my ears scarlet. When I pushed down with my feet in my shoes I could hear the blood squishing. I had to get out of there.

It was better in the jungle. There were others with razor-blade brains. Not as many as you might think, but quite a few. We'd volunteer for night patrol. We stayed to ourselves. We didn't do drugs or drink alcohol. We chain smoked cigarettes, which we were told was bad for our health. We laughed and laughed. Most of us volunteered for a second tour. A good 30% of us made it home again.

A mother with an angel of a daughter no older than four just walked past my car.

"Mommy, why is that man sitting in that hot car smoking cigarettes?" she asked.

"Hush, Grace," said her mother.

I thought it was a fair question.

Hail Mary, full of grace, remind me to tell you about my time in the seminary. I laughed there, too. I laughed so non-stop hard that they drummed me out the door at 3 a.m. into a blinding blizzard. "God's speed," said the Father Superior.

The next morning on their way to sunrise service they discovered crimson footprints in the snow. The footprints crossed the grounds and passed through the holy arch out into the world. The snow had fallen all night, but it did not fill the footprints. There was talk of miracles, but the Father Superior squelched it. He brought in a bulldozer and a dump truck and had the snow removed. They dropped it into the Connecticut River and the river turned crimson. Scientists wrote it off as an outbreak of a rare form of algae, and the matter was dropped.

I joined up at Fort Jackson in Columbia, South Carolina. They asked me what I wanted to do and I said kill. "Right," said the enlistment sergeant., and put me on a bus to Texas.

Humungous, Lord of the Wasteland

Knock me down and roll me over. Two beef-and-bean burritos from Taco Bell on a hot June night after a two-hour nap. Not the lifestyle that leads to an Honors Program appearance.

Nap's not the word for it. There is no word for it. Surfacing from a heat-stroke exhaustion sleep after a blistering day working in the sun, not sure if it's morning or night, head spinning with threat dream, seven in the evening, every bone in my body aching--those are the words for it. One of those vulnerable moments when you think, "I can't keep going on like this."

A glass of distilled water, check the email on the way out the door, and someone wants me to accompany them to hear Adrienne Rich talk poetry at the university tomorrow night, an event sponsored by the Honors Program that has no truck with Taco-Bell burrito eaters.

It's quite a landscape up there in my head. Something to make The Road Warrior look like a stroll through the park. I started the day up here on this hill at 6 a.m. with a coffee, a cigarette and Suzuki. "The way to study Zen is not verbal. Just open yourself and give up everything," it says at the beginning of the section of *Not Always So* titled *Practicing Zen.* I read that and closed the book. What else do I need to know? I drank my coffee looking out over the valley at the Cascade range in the distance while Suzuki drove the Mighty Humungous, Lord of the Wasteland, back out into the desert. I drove down off the hill, and the day began reeling me in, dropping me into its catch basket, and by 5 p.m. hammering me unconscious. I'm not sure if I'm striving for balance here or verging on pulling all the stops and riding out into the desert to take on Humungous and his filthy lot single-handed.

I met Adrienne Rich once, many years ago at a party in a fashionable Seattle neighborhood. I was running with Jesse Bernstein the poet and John Harter the artist, both suicides-in-waiting. We got wind of the party at the Comet Tavern and showed up uninvited. I remember being out on the lawn going nose-to-nose with Ms. Rich, and I remember her going silent and getting that steely look in her eyes that I'd seen in Ferlinghetti's eyes a few years earlier in San Francisco in a similar standoff situation. "Now you did it, Bennett," Bukowski said then. "No City Lights book for you."

I think I'll pass on paying money to go hear Ms. Rich talk. I'll continue to fuel up on Taco-Bell burritos, and one of these days I'll rip that steel mask off the Mighty Humungous and-- lo! There'll be Adrienne Rich!

I have to go now. Suzuki is growing impatient. "Ah, Grasshopper," he's saying. "What a piece of work you are!"

All My Friends
Are Going to Be
Strangers

They're always on the move, they're in Saint Petersburg and then off they go to Stockholm. Some stay in 5-star hotels, others in tents, but they all take pictures with their cell phones and send them to each other email.

I used to sneer at people taking pictures with cell phones, but now I too have a cell phone that takes pictures. For weeks I took pictures of everything under the sun and the phone gobbled them up. Then a young girl who's flunking high-school English, sweet and soft-spoken, murmured, "Could I see it for a second?"

I didn't understand why she was flunking English, she spoke it perfectly fine. I handed her my phone and in nothing flat there were all the pictures I though were lost, lined up and labeled in sequential order.

"Well will you look at that!" I said.

She smiled. "Would you like to put them on your computer so you can send them to your friends?" she asked.

"Yes!" I said. "That would be great!" Here was a window of opportunity, a chance to redeem myself with my friends in Paris and Rome and the few still in Saint Petersburg--they'd been steadily sending me cell-phone pictures, but when I didn't reciprocate, the number of pictures tapered off, and then the emails themselves began to dwindle.

"Do you have Bluetooth?" asked the girl.

"I beg your pardon?" I said. I thought maybe my breath

was bad or that my teeth were changing color. I was afraid that now she wouldn't help me get back in touch with my friends.

"On your computer, I mean," she said. "You have it on your cell phone--see?" She pushed some buttons and brought up an icon. "Is your computer on?" she said. "Do you mind?"

She sat down at my computer and with a few clicks brought up the same icon that was on my cell phone.

And then she did something that drove it home to me like a spike through a vampire's heart that I was cut off not from one world but two--the world I was born into and this world that had replaced it. And that in between the two there must have been another, a transitional world that I missed completely. She punched in a series of commands on the cell phone, and the pictures I'd taken began appearing on the computer.

"There," she said, when she was done. "Now you can send them to your friends."

They were meaningless pictures, the product of someone fumbling with a technology beyond his grasp. But I sent them anyway, and gradually my friends began emailing again, asking cautiously if I had any travel plans.

The Journal of Amazing Grace

Bix Beiderbecke standing on a pier in Davenport hears Louis Armstrong blasting away on his trumpet from the deck of a riverboat and goes out and buys a cornet.

Years later, sitting in the colored section of a segregated theater, Louis Armstrong hears Bix Beiderbecke, and after the show he meets him at the stage door and drags him off to an apartment in Queens where the two of them blow their horns all night until the sun comes up. They can't play together in public, this black boy and this white boy, these giants of jazz.

Louis Armstrong smoked a lot of reefer, which didn't seem to slow him down none, and Bix Beiderbecke drank a lot of alcohol, which killed him.

Actually, as any hardcore A.A. knows, drinking is but a symptom of the problem--Bix Beiderbecke died of a broken heart. He was a victim of racism. What might have saved his life is if he'd been born black.

James Baldwin turned Nelson Algren away from his motel door behind which he was entertaining black militants. James Baldwin didn't know what Louis Armstrong knew.

Still, don't trust anyone who walks around with a sheet over his head.

The Great White Hope

They said he was uppity, that he transgressed the values chiseled in stone. They took issue with his shrugged shoulder, his bemused smile, his raised eyebrow, his inappropriate yawn when they said something important, his sledgehammer right that came out of nowhere like thunder and laid them low, one after the other. They couldn't tolerate his being educated without having been educated, his playing the cello, his tinkerings that turned into inventions, the white women who swam around him like mermaids. But mostly they were outraged that they let him become the heavyweight champion of the world.

Even black men disapproved of him, the giants of his day, Booker T. Washington and Edward DuBois, but no one could stop him, no one could bring him down, he rolled over them all. He didn't seem to realize he was black, and he certainly didn't think he was white.

"I'm Jack Johnson," he said. "End of story."

When he'd had enough, he ran his car off the road at 70 mph and left as abruptly as he'd appeared, shadow boxing his way into heaven.

Anita O'Day

There are lots of checkmates and fool's mates and a good
number of stalemates and forfeits in life, but no *en passants.*
Once something passes you by, it's gone forever.

My son went that route, marched right out of my life, but I
wound up with his daughter, and chess has no name for second
chances.

She's staying with me now, healing from the road, but
she has a deeper pain that no one can get to, so deep it turns
physical, a knot in her stomach. She's fierce proud, proud and
strong, too strong, she hasn't learned how to let strength take
on resilience. She's only twenty.

It's 104 degrees, I cut work short at noon and my
granddaughter and I draped blankets over the west windows
to keep the heat out, cranked up the floor fans, and stuck in
a DVD--*Anita O'Day: The Life of a Jazz Singer.* And there it
was in so many ways, a mirror image of my granddaughter, the
strength and the pride.

Anita O'Day, who everyone who knows about these things
ranks with Billie Holiday, Ella Fitzgerald and Sarah Vaughan
as the top jazz divas of an era. She kicked heroin and alcohol
and pot and who knows what else on her own. She died at 87 in
November of 2006.

"I want to sing like that," my granddaughter said
afterward, and then, "I'm going back over the mountains to my
mom's tomorrow. She needs me."

I'm caught off guard by my reaction, uncut disappointment.
It shows on my face. My granddaughter reads it, and over
her face comes a mix of happiness that I'll miss her and pain

because she doesn't want to see me lonely. This is the pain that is hurting her, down under a hard-boiled veneer just like Anita O'Day's--feeling the pain of others and being able to do nothing about it.

Later I'm on the computer, tapped into some photos of crazy artists and poets from my past. I call her in and scroll through the photos, and when I'm done she says, "I want to have pictures like that."

"You will," I said. "You're still young."

"No," she says. "People aren't like that anymore," and we both grow silent.

Bonding with Phantoms

I identify
as much with
Major Tom
as anyone
& he
doesn't even
exist.

The Major Tom Fiasco

Fiasco may be too strong. Misunderstanding perhaps. Mass confusion. Well, mild perplexity. A kaleidoscope of hope and fear.

I want to supercharge rainbows of color into a drab existence. Not mine but the one mine is mired in. Yours too, but if you don't realize it, it hardly matters.

I hold the palm of my hand over the candle flame. "This is not what candles were made for!" I'm admonished. "This is not romance!"

I know that much. It's a form of discipline. A way to learn not to cry out and give away my position when the pain torques. If I had my way I'd turn the whole world to metaphor.

What information I possess is like a pored-over smörgåsbord. The mangled remains of what's eatable. Tidbits and scraps. When you travel fast and non-stop, odd things from everywhere cling to you.

People in the know write back that David Bowie, who created Major Tom, is a musical genius. One in-the-know individual made mention of Peter Shilling, a German who did his own spin-off on Major Tom, which threw another turnip into the potpourri of my mishmash information.

Those who never heard of Major Tom grow agitated when David Bowie is mentioned. The more unknowns get tossed into the salad, the more vehement they become. "You're making things up because you can't handle reality!" they scream.

I can't handle screaming. I let out some tether and float off into space.

"Come back here!" they scream. "You can't just *float away!*"

Someone else has a hunch that Major Tom was my commanding officer in the army, and they want to know what took him out. Something took him out if he no longer exists like it says in the poem, Shard, whatever the hell I'm calling them these days. Was it in Nam? Somalia? Afghanistan? Was he still a major? A colonel? Maybe a one-star general? This individual is a frustrated historian who longs to take part in a literary seminar and so launches deeper into inference: Am I still a soldier at heart? Am I about to wage war?

"What right do you have to bombard people with this esoteric blather?" ask the totally out of it. "What right do you have to write this way?"

Let's see now. When I went to school at the age of seven, I could read and write. When the nun got through with me, I no longer could do either. I had to start from scratch, and this is how far I've got.

The right to write? What goes around comes around, unless you kill it dead.

We live in a culture shattered like a huge pane of glass. I'm just a clown with a tube of super glue, sweeping up the shards and pasting them together willy-nilly while longing to float into space.

Me and Major Tom, off on the great adventure.

An Act of Contrition
(from the ongoing saga of Major Tom)

Do you know what that means, having someone destroy your ability to read and write at the age of seven?

It means God is not on your side.

It means the nun was light years ahead of her time. Three days alone in a closed room with Tokyo Rose and she would have had a signed confession and Rose never would have had the chance to set up a flower shop in Chicago. The Second World War would have ended sooner and the war on terror would not have been necessary if only the nun had directed her powers elsewhere back when she was beating your brains out in the first grade.

It means you're the reason the mass is now said in English.

It means there may come a knock on your door at 3 a.m. and you'll be taken away to answer hard questions. Like who was it taught you to read and write again and who are you working for?

We know better now. We're in a perpetual state of red alert and we'll stay there until democracy blankets the earth. You're not going anywhere, you and your sidekick Major Tom.

An act of contrition might win you some leniency, but not much, and not until we've got a list of names two pages long.

The Morphing of Major Tom

Both David Bowie and Peter Schilling have passed word down through anonymous channels that I've got no claim on Major Tom. That Major Tom is an outer-space loner and I'm a brain-damaged Catholic. That I wouldn't last a minute floating in outer space cut off from Ground Control. That I should crawl up in a corner.

Well. What do they know? Does Frankenstein belong to his maker? Is Rush Limbaugh a child of Christ? Is Christ the son of God or a Major Tom incarnation?

Perhaps David Bowie is Saint John the Baptist with his head in a pretty girl's lap. Perhaps Peter Schilling should brush up on his English. Perhaps Major Tom is a white dove perched on my shoulder like a parrot. Perhaps I'm a prophet caught up in unusual circumstances. Perhaps you're not buying this, but I'll tell you what--I'm losing patience.

See those dark clouds on the distant horizon? Hear the rumbling thunder?

This is Major Tom to Ground Control: the jig is up.

The Street

We're all seeking truth. We're all seeking answers. We're all looking for a way out, a way in, an anchor with links as thick as giant sausage to drop and weather the storm. And then reality strikes, the messy unpredictable here-and-now.

People talking war. People talking carnage. People talking the abstraction of distant suffering. You don't know what six German riot police are until they kick in your door, and then they're not German, they're not even riot police, they're six men with license. From the moment the door splinters off its hinges and your wife starts screaming with her hands over her ears and the two English vagrants you've been harboring make a dash for the window, generalities and abstractions and speculations get vaporized and life explodes into a shower of micro-seconds.

***

The Pentagon March, 1967. Face-to-face with a row of bayoneted rifles and gas masks with 19-year-old boys behind them. A girl sticks a rose down a barrel, someone barks a command, and the boys move forward in the short-thrust position. Someone grabs a rifle, someone gives a shove, Norman Mailer has come and gone, Dick Gregory has been rushed to the hospital at the tail end of his protest fast, and then they fire the tear gas.

Things shatter into myriad particulars. You and Grant slide down a hillside and come face to mask with a soldier who is pointing his bayonet at you, and you're thinking not about the war or justice or equal rights but that this kid doesn't know Grant. You've been here with him before, in New Orleans, on the streets of Brussels, this has nothing to do with McNamara or Mailer, with the Nam, this is personal, and like a swift jungle cat Grant wrenches the rifle out the the boy's hands, flings it aside, and rips off the mask.

The kid is scared and has no idea what he's doing. "I'm sorry," he says, choking on the gas, and--eyes stinging and throats burning--Grant and I laugh. Grant gives the kid a bear hug and we haul ass out of there.

***

I'm parked in my work van up on the hill at 6 a.m., the only vehicle up here, the window rolled down to let in the fresh morning air, drinking coffee and smoking and writing this, when a low rider pulls up.

A low rider? In Ellensburg? *On the hill at 6 a.m.?*

The tinted window goes down and a black chick says, "You got a cigarette?"

There's an Arab-looking guy with a gold chain around his neck behind the wheel, and a blond in the back with plucked eyebrows. The four of us are taking readings like crazy.

"I roll my own," I say.

"Huh," says the black chick.

The window goes up and the low rider backs slowly in behind me.

I keep writing. I write what just happened and then I study the low rider in the rear-view mirror. I get out of the van and walk back there. The passenger-side window comes down about halfway and I walk around and hold out a cigarette. This isn't in the script, and that gives me the upper hand.

"I don't smoke rollies," says the black chick, but when I

continue to hold it out, she takes it, reluctantly. "Do you smoke rollies?" she says to the girl in the back.

"I'll smoke it," the girl says, and the black chick hands it back. The girl twists one end of the cigarette like it's a joint and I hand in a lighter.

The Arab-looking guy has both hands on the wheel and is looking straight out the windshield.

The girl in back lights up, leans forward, and hands the lighter back out. "Thanks," she says.

"No problem," I say, and walk back to the van.

I've got all the information I need to rest easy.

***

Years ago, in San Francisco, me and my friend Gary, whose whole life is an abstraction, were driving down a deserted street off Broadway around midnight after a night of drinking when a woman sprang out from behind a hedge and came running toward the car, waving her hands frantically.

Gary stopped, put the car in park, and with the motor still running, got out. I took one look at the woman, the way she was dressed, the way her eyes didn't match her arm waving, and my eyes began darting around. Sure enough, here's this guy coming around the other end of the hedge, one arm stiff at his side, a pistol in his hand.

"Get in!" I shout at Gary. "Get the fuck out of here!"

"She needs help!" Gary says. He still hasn't seen the man with the pistol.

"Fuck she does!" I say. "There's a guy with a gun!"

Gary freezes in place, his eyes glazed--he was rolled in the Fillmore just a week earlier. I reach out, yank him back behind the wheel, put the car in gear, get my foot on the gas and floor it. We go careening down the street, the driver's side door flapping wildly, Gary steering reflexively.

I twist around and look out the rear window. The man and woman are standing side-by-side in the middle of the street, the woman with her hands on her hips, the man with his arm still stiff at his side, holding the pistol.

***

If you've spent any time on the street, all this makes sense to you.

The street is where things get processed at lightning speed.

The street is a state of mind.

People who don't know the street are fair game, and they get what they deserve.

Working the Garter

one

The Red Garter was a coast-to-coast chain of banjo bars back in the 60s and 70s. They even had one in Florence, Italy. I worked the French Quarter Garter on the corner of Bourbon and St. Peter.

The ones we enjoyed throwing out the most were the loud-mouth karate guys. Wilcox, a street fighter down from the Bronx, would walk up to one of them and stand there with his hands dangling at his sides while the guy went through his gyrations. Then Wilcox would punch him in the Adam's Apple and down he'd go. A couple of waiters would drag him through the swinging doors and toss him in the gutter. Wilcox had the fastest hands I ever saw.

The roughnecks in from the drilling rigs were a tough lot to handle. Even tougher were the off-shore divers. But the only guys we ever refused to tangle with was a hockey team down from Canada. We called the cops when they started busting up chairs and tables, and even the cops didn't want to mess with them.

two

It was Mardi Gras and I was working the front bar. It was in the afternoon, and the place was packed wall-to-wall, the banjos and washboard and piano going at it full tilt.

Waiters shouldered their way through the crowd and either called out their orders in a loud voice or used hand signals we'd worked out. I'd just served up a big order and was scanning the floor and I see this guy five or six tables deep in the crowd bring a beer pitcher around in a wide sweep and take off half of another's guy's face who was sitting across from him. The guy fell to the floor like a sack of rocks.

No one except the people at the table noticed. The music kept blasting away and the crowd kept roaring and the guy who'd done the damage began working his way through the crowd, heading for the door.

I high-signed Tank who they'd brought in from Dallas to work the door for Mardi Gras. Tank wore a bright red orchestra jacket and a string tie over a grayed-out white shirt. His hair was orange and slicked back. He was shaped like a square and must have weighed 300 lbs. He and the guy trying to get out of there came face to face right in front of the bar. Tank bent his right arm up at the elbow fist out and with a short jab like a jackhammer splattered the guy's nose all over his face; he went down, and Tank went back to the door, adjusting his string tie with one hand and smoothing back his greasy hair with the other.

three

On Saturday nights they used to have beer guzzling contests. Three or four college guys would get up on the bandstand with a pitcher of beer each and go at it.

One night a fat sailor already so drunk his eyes were vacant got up there with the college kids. He drained his pitcher in one go and then went over face first onto a long table directly in front of the bandstand. The table shattered.

There were some lawyer types at the table with hot sexy ladies. They all jumped up, the ladies screaming and the lawyers brushing at their expensive suits that were splattered with beer.

By the time me and two other waiters got there, the sailor was on his feet again. He ripped the blouse off one of the ladies and groped at her breasts. He moved like he was submerged in molasses.

He was incredibly strong. The other two waiters each grabbed and arm, and the sailor shook them off like flies, sent them crashing into the wreckage of the shattered table.

The bartender vaulted over the bar with a blackjack and brought it down on the back of the sailor's head. The sailor turned slowly, lifted the bartender off his feet, and tossed him in with the waiters. Then he turned his attention to me.

I started talking. Anything that came into my head. I talked about being a kid and having bullies pick on me until one day I said fuck this and laid into the captain of the soccer team in the crowded hallway between classes and got expelled. The sailor got a vague smile on his face.

While this was going on the waiters and the bartender crawled out of the wreckage. One of the waiters put his finger to his lips and then went down on his hands and knees behind the sailor. I kept right on talking, took a step in, and shoved. The sailor went over the waiter like an elephant falling off a cliff. The bartender and me and the other two waiters each got an arm or a leg, and with a lot of effort, managed to drag the sailor out into the street. Then we ran back inside and bolted the doors. The place had all but emptied out, and the band had stopped playing. The cops came, and it took six of them to get the sailor into the back of a squad car, beating on him with billy clubs the whole time.

The rest of the night the place was like a morgue. We closed early and went down to the Seven Seas to drink.

four

I was on the door. It was early and I hadn't started barking people inside yet. I stood there smoking and watching the tourists stream by. In the street at the curb was a corndog stand, this thing shaped like a corndog with bicycle wheels on either side and a bar at one end to push it along. The top swung open, and inside were trays of steaming corndogs and hot dogs and sauerkraut.

A lanky guy in jeans and work boots who had bayou written all over him was walking up to place an order when this middle-aged tourist with short hair and glasses wearing penny loafers and a shirt with a button-down collar stepped in front of him. The lanky guy tapped him on the shoulder and said something, and the tourist turned his head and said something back and then turned away again.

He brought the thing out of a side pocket of his windbreaker--a curved blade welded to about three inches of metal rod with a perpendicular wood dowel on the end of it that served as a grip handle. The sort of tool a dock worker might use to cut twine or sink into certain types of cargo to move it easier. The corndog man saw it too, and he stepped way back.

Everything went into slow motion. The tourist turned, and he saw it. He began walking in rapid little steps around and around the corndog stand, the lanky guy loping along behind him until he caught up. He grabbed him by the hair, yanked his head back, and slit his throat from ear to ear.

The tourist didn't even cry out, but blood was spurting out of his throat, and he went down. The lanky guy slipped the blade back into his pocket and faded into crowd.

five

I got off work and went down to an invite-only gig where the Jefferson Airplane was playing after doing a concert. I drank a bottle of tequila in about an hour and went a little crazy. I turned over I don't know how many tables on my way to the door. When I came through the door I was yelling and a short nicely dressed guy said, "You want to fuck with *me?*"

"I'll fuck with anyone!" I roared, and from all reports this guy brought the punch up from the sidewalk, busted my nose, and laid me out cold.

I came to in the emergency room at Charity Hospital, slumped in a chair against a wall in a long line of chairs with black guys in them who'd been shot or stabbed.

When they were done with me, I went down to the river and sat on the rocks, smoking and watching the sun come up.

six

We weren't open for business yet but the swinging doors were tied back to air the place out. This guy came in, walked straight up to the piano player who was sitting on a stool with his back to the bar with a drink in his hand, pulled out a pistol and shot him point-blank in the chest.

The shot made a popping sound, not loud at all, and the piano player slumped back against the bar, gurgling. "Oh," he kept saying. "Oh, oh, oh..."

There wasn't much blood. Just a crimson spot on his shirt, small at first, but it kept getting bigger.

seven

I got out of New Orleans. Moved to San Francisco. Worked the post office days and the Red Garter on Broadway nights.

The place next door to the Garter back then was a Go-Go bar frequented almost exclusively by Filipinos. One night while I was working the door three Latinos went in there around midnight. Pretty soon they came back out again with six Filipinos all over them. They had knives and broken bottles, and they slashed up those three Latinos good. Even after they were down on the pavement they didn't stop. There was blood everywhere. I yelled in for the bartender to dial 9-1-1. You don't step into something like that single-handed.

The Filipinos finally went back inside. A paddy wagon and two squad cars showed up. They tossed the three Latinos in the paddy wagon and drove off.

The next day I slept through my morning shift at the post office for the third time in a month. I put in a call to the manager at the New Orleans Garter. He offered to pay my plane fare down plus salary and a bonus to work Mardi Gras, which was a week off.

I flew out that afternoon.

Fear & Understanding

It scares me
what you write
a woman said
recently.
I don't
understand it.

You understand it
more than you
realize
if it
scares you
I said,
& then she looked
really scared.

Drive By

It's when the writing turns to music that a lot of readers refuse to read further.

"Music!" they cry. "Like John Cage and a shattered window?"

"Yes!" I say. "Right on! Hop up on the hay ride and let me take your clothes off!"

And away they scamper.

***

I'm simply gathering steam. Building my biceps. Getting ready for the Big Ride in the Sky, a Super Shard the length of a novel. The *Journal of Albion Moonlight* and *Naked Lunch* rolled into one, poured into a narrow-necked bottle like gasoline and then stuffed with the rag of Gregory Corso's left sock. Sparked with some e.e. cummings and tossed thru the first window I drive by.

Drive By. That's what I'll call it. See how easy titles roll down the chute?

That's a good note to end on.

Photo by Jackie Bangs

JOHN BENNETT writes with a tiny, fist-sized stuffed bear in sorcerer's garb on top of his computer. Not too many years back he wrote on a wide-carriage manual typewriter. On the road he writes on legal pads and napkins. The bear is a gift from his granddaughter, a perceptive, jewel of a girl with laughing eyes.

Veteran small-press poet and writer, editor and publisher of the legendary Vagabond Press.

A brace of fine books to his credit, including the novel Bodo that came out in New York, London and Prague editions and got nominated for the Los Angeles Times Book of the Year Award. Go to the Hcolom Press web site for a complete listing of published books along with synopses and feedback: www.hcolompress.com/Books.html

Began writing Shards in the mid-nineties and has never looked back.

ABOUT THE LUMMOX PRESS

Lummox Press was created in 1994 by RD Armstrong. It began as a self-publishing/DIY imprint for poetry by RD. Several chapbooks were published and in late 1995 it began publishing the Lummox Journal, a monthly small/ underground press lit-arts zine. Available primarily by sub- scription, the LJ continued it's exploration of the "creative process" until its demise as a print mag in 2006.

During its eleven year existence, this tiny mag with the big name, interviewed poets, musicians and artists (over 100 in all) about how they do what they do. Hundreds of poems were also published in its pages. Poets like *Todd Moore, Lyn Lifshin, Gerald Locklin, Holly Prado, L.A. Bogen, Linda Lerner, Scott Wannberg, Philomene Long, John Thomas* and *RD Armstrong*, to name a few, appeared regularly within its pages. It was hailed as one of the best monthly's in the small press.

In 1998, Lummox began publishing the Little Red Book series, and continues to do so today. To date there are some 63 titles in the series (as of 2009) and this year a collection of poems from the first decade of the series has been published under the title, **The Long Way Home** (2009).

Lummox also published limited edition books such as **The Wren Notebook** by Rick Smith (2000) and **Last Call: The Legacy of Charles Bukowski** (2004). More recently, Lummox published a set of four titles from its founder, RD Armstrong: **On/Off the Beaten Path** (a trio of long poems about road trips taken in 1999, 2000 and 2001 including the epic poem RoadKill – which John Berbrich said was "the best post 9-11 writing I've seen"), **Fire and Rain – Se- lected Poems 1993-2007** Volumes 1 & 2 and **El Pagano and**

Other Twisted Tales (a collection of short stories and flash fiction). All were published in 2008. In late 2008 Lummox began publishing the *RESPECT* series starting with *John Yamrus'* **New and Selected Poems**. This was followed by *Todd Moore's* **The Riddle of the Wooden Gun** (2009); **Sea Trails** by *Pris Campbell* (2009) and **Down This Crooked Road – Modern Poetry from the Road Less Traveled** edited by *RD Armstrong and William Taylor, Jr.* (2009). These books are available directly from the Lummox Press via the website: www.lummoxpress.com or at Lummox c/o PO Box 5301 San Pedro, CA 90733. There are also E-Book versions of most titles available.

Please visit the website to read selections from these titles as well as peruse the many other titles/articles published by the Lummox Press.

Ask your independent bookstore to carry these titles, since Lummox only deals with independent book stores like Powell's of Portland, OR; The Book Collector of Sacramento, CA or Moe's of Berkeley, CA.

Together with Chris Yeseta (Layout and Art Direction since 1997), **RD** continues to publish books that are both striking in their looks as well as their content…you'd think he was aping Black Sparrow, but he is merely trying to produce the best books he can for his clients, the poets, and their customers, you, the reader.

www.ingramcontent.com/pod-product-compliance
Lightning Source LLC
Chambersburg PA
CBHW050758250626
47155CB00005B/2126